T0104465

Adventures at Hi-Lonesome Ranch

The Magic Cabin, Book Two

Jane Wyche Wofford

WESTBOW®
PRESS
A DIVISION OF THOMAS NELSON
& ZONDERVAN

Illustrations by Nancy Utter.

WestBow Press books may be ordered through booksellers or by contacting:

WestBow Press
A Division of Thomas Nelson & Zondervan
1663 Liberty Drive
Bloomington, IN 47403
www.westbowpress.com
1 (866) 928-1240

ISBN: 978-1-4908-1824-5 (sc)
ISBN: 978-1-4908-1825-2 (e)

Library of Congress Control Number: 2013922050

Printed in the United States of America.

WestBow Press rev. date: 01/14/2014

CONTENTS

CHAPTER 1 NEW SCHOOL BLUES..................................1
CHAPTER 2 BULLIES, TEACHERS AND FRIENDS ...11
CHAPTER 3 NEW SCHOOL SURPRISES 19
CHAPTER 4 FIRE...28
CHAPTER 5 OUTDOOR SCHOOL 37
CHAPTER 6 ADVENTURE FIRE-OUT 46
CHAPTER 7 TEDDY BEAR DAY 55
CHAPTER 8 FIREFIGHTERS LIFELINE......................64
CHAPTER 9 THE ENEMY ATTACKS 72
CHAPTER 10 FAMILY SKI ADVENTURES 81
CHAPTER 11 MOUNTAIN CABIN CHRISTMAS.........91
CHAPTER 12 A NEW FRIEND 99
CHAPTER 13 THE SECRET GIFT.............................108
CHAPTER 14 MINDY'S PRISON 116
CHAPTER 15 THE MUSTANG TRAIL 125
CHAPTER 16 RUNNING MUSTANGS 133
CHAPTER 17 THE BIG POW-WOW 141
CHAPTER 18 TIN CUP BURGERS 151
CHAPTER 19 MINDY FACES DANGER.......................161
CHAPTER 20 MINDY'S WINS HER SPURS 171

PROLOGUE

The lone cowboy rode out of the woods and into a large clearing. At the other end of the clearing stood an old log cabin and nearby was a log barn built dug-out style into a low hill. He could hear a stream rushing somewhere close by.

The man was surprised that the barn and cabin were still standing. He was following his great grandpa's journal that he had written many years ago, on his journey west. And in Grandpa Nathaniel Wyche's journal he had written about this exact spot, where he had camped for one night.

"Surely, no one has lived here for awhile," Nathaniel had written.

"It looks vacant and run down, but a mighty find place to camp!"

"I thought these buildings would be rotted and on the ground," Nate, the young cowboy thought. But in the late afternoon light, he could see people moving around in the house. Outside the barn were two four wheelers.

Nate nudged his horse forward and tied the reigns to the railing on the front porch. He stepped up to the rough sawn front door and raised his hand to knock. Loud barking announced his arrival, and a young boy opened the door.

"Howdy," Nate said in his friendly Texas voice. "Your folks home?" A bearded man in worn jeans and sturdy boots came up behind the boy. He had wild white hair and bushy eyebrows, and a face that had friendly eyes, but they held caution as well.

After a few minutes of talk with the stranger, Doc and Josh gave each other a mental thumbs up and invited him in. The rest of the folks sitting around the table were dishing out a meal that smelled delicious. He repeated some of the things that he had told Doc and Josh outside, and everyone started asking him questions.

"Let the man catch his breath," the woman at the stove said. "Why don't you sit down and have dinner with us, Nathan…did I say your name right?"

"It just Nate, mam, but I don't mean to impose."

"There's always plenty of food," she said. "Never can tell who's gonna drop in and need filling up."

Doc began to introduce each one around the table. "You already met Josh. And Mindy is the next oldest and over there is Karilynn. The extra seat at the table is for their Dad, who is off on business."

"And the lady at the stove lady is Sherry Cunningham, the Best Cook in Texas and Colorado. While Dad is away, she is the boss of this outfit," Doc said, finishing the introductions.

"Well, now," Nate spoke up. "I am Nate Wyche from Texas. My great grandfather camped here one night back in 1881 when he was on his way out West looking for adventure. I have his journal and am following his route to California. That's how I come to be here tonight."

After a delicious dinner, they invited Nate to bed down in the cabin. "Thanks," he said, "but I am trying to follow Grandpa Nathaniel's travels in all aspects."

"Got it," Doc said, and everyone else nodded in understanding.

"But before I go pitch camp, Grandpa wrote in his journal about spending the night here. Would you like to hear it?"

They all nodded enthusiastically and then moved to the living room. Nate dusted off an old leather journal and began to read.

> *"I camped last night next to a creek and an old log cabin. There was also a dugout barn. Both looked lonely and empty. A hoot owl woke me up out of a deep sleep. The moon was up and it was bright as day. I looked at the buildings again. Now they didn't look empty and vacant at all, just quiet and waiting. Mystery was in the air and it felt like the buildings were hiding secrets that they wanted to share with me. I laughed at myself in the morning. The barn and cabin looked like ordinary old buildings. After breakfast, I saddled up to ride off. I looked back over my shoulder at the edge of the clearing. I felt the Mystery once again in the air, so thick it seemed like I could touch it. The old cabin was calling me to venture in and share it's secrets. I spoke out loud and said, "I have other fish to fry, Old Cabin. I'm heading west for my adventures. You will have to keep waiting for someone else to come along to share your Mysteries and secrets."*

Nate closed the book and looked around. Mom and Doc started asking him questions, but all the kids sat very quiet. "So have found any mysteries and secrets here," Nate laughed, as he studied the quiet kids.

"Well, it depends on how you describe mysteries and secrets?" Josh replied cautiously. "We sure have had a lot of adventures since we moved here."

All the three kids looked at the floor and tried not to laugh. Nate noticed the bear in the little girl's lap with his paw over his mouth. Two bees sat like statues on the grandfather clock, not flitting a wing or making a sound. Nate took it all in and wondered what the heck they were not telling him.

When they all said good night, Nate promised to get in touch after he finished his western journey. The next morning he had ridden on.

CHAPTER 1

NEW SCHOOL BLUES

Doc and Josh leaned back against a smooth rock under a huge pine tree as Josh described an argument with his mother about his new school in Monte Vista. The old man with wild white hair and bushy eyebrows gazed at the young boy with concern.

"I like it here just fine, Doc, I really do! These woods, our log cabin, and some of my new friends are a lot more exciting than living in a hot Texas city," Josh reassured Doc, as he stroked the head of a dog with enormous puppy feet. "But I didn't bargain for going to a new school. I hate going to new schools. Mom promised that she would check into home schooling for us. That way we would have school right in our cabin."

"You'll make friends fast, Josh," the man said. "Stuck out here in the woods, you'll never get to know the kids in town. Sisters are nice, but you'll want friends of your own, football, girls and…"

"Yeah, Mom says that too, Doc," Josh interrupted rudely. He picked up a pine cone and chucked it toward a squirrel who did not seem bothered by humans in his backyard. Hank, his dog, sat up and sniffed the air, half-heartedly tugging at the hold that Josh had on his collar. Doc's dog, Killer, slept close by his owner's side.

"*You kids will need a 'social life'*," Josh quoted his mother, "whatever that is. Hanging out with a bunch of kids I don't know is not my idea of fun. And trying to make friends in a school where everyone has grown up together sounds like a nightmare." Josh concluded with a moan.

"You three kids can take on the new school together. Your mom, bless her heart, always looks at things as an adventure. Two new girls and a jock will make quite a splash at the Monte Vista School, of that I'm sure," encouraged Doc.

"Oh boy! A new school, a social life with strangers, and dragging my little sisters with me to school. I'm really gonna' love this adventure." complained Josh as he headed for home.

***

As Josh headed home, Doc returned to his cabin upstream from the Cunninghams. He was surprised to find a stranger with short dark hair on his front porch. Now, if you go to the movies, you would immediately identify Doc's visitor. He wore a plain blue suit with matching blue tie over a starched white shirt.

He had FBI written all over him. It looked as if he had stepped out of a current TV series. He stood ramrod straight with the obvious bulge over his left hip.

Not being a big fan of trespassers, Doc immediately asked what he was doing on private property. The agent introduced himself and began to explain why he was there.

Hiding in the nearby trees were two large animals. One had huge flat horns that covered his entire head. His female companion stood nearby. Two large bumble bees sat on the horns of the male moose. Moose and bees quietly listened to the conversation.

Doc had a worried expression on his face, his fierce eyebrows drawn together. His typically friendly eyes were dark and anxious. Even Killer, his faithful companion, stood alert at his side.

The nearby critters caught wind-blown words of the conversation. The names Mindy, Josh and Karilynn were repeated several times and seemed to be connected to the word *danger*. The word prince also floated through the conversation. Even if the critters didn't understand much of the animated talking, they did understand that the Cunningham kids and Doc seemed to be in danger.

"Well, we'll just have to keep an eye on them," the bigger moose replied slowly. "I'll bet Doc will be watching out too." whispered Manners in a mooseey voice to the small group. A "Bruummble" was all they heard from Fifty Point as he moved back into the forest.

***

Mindy sat on a fence railing watching the cowboy named Charlie and a new horse in the training arena. Of the three Cunningham kids, she had fought coming to their new Colorado home the hardest. She was not looking forward to a new school either, but that was the last thing on her mind right now.

The summer was almost over and Mindy had fallen in love. *Horses!* Mindy ate, slept, read, and thought about nothing but horses. All summer long she had bugged her Mom into taking her to grandpa's ranch, The Hi-Lonesome Horse Training Center as often as she could.

In fact, that had been the way that Mindy had fought off the loneliness that she felt having left her home and friends behind in Austin. She would catch a ride to the ranch, where she would hang around the barn, helping out with small chores. Nothing seemed like a chore when she was taking care of the horses she now considered friends. Their warm muzzles and soft whinnies encouraged her through many a lonely day. And that was the story of how horses had become Mindy's new passion.

It would seem that Mindy was the luckiest girl in Colorado. She had a grandpa who owned a beautiful ranch which was well known for training top horses. She loved horses, and her grandpa was in the Horse Business. It was an ideal equation for her to live happily ever after.

But her dreams were clouded by Grandpa Cunningham. Mindy and her family had moved from Texas to Colorado to live in an old cabin twelve miles from ranch headquarters. They had never met their grandpa before moving. It took no time at all to discover that he was a man who did not relish human contact, didn't understand children, and had no desire for any kids to interfere with his normal routines.

"You gotta understand. He gets along better with the animals than he does with people," their great Aunt Netta had informed them. Aunt Netta and Charlie, who lived at the ranch, always provided a warm welcome whenever the Cunningham family visited. But Grandpa only passed through with a grumpy greeting on his way out the door.

Mindy suspected that it was Charlie who had coaxed Grandpa into letting her spend so much time on the ranch. She had followed

Charlie around and, when he found her willing to stay out of the way and help out as needed, he seemed glad to have her company.

"Hey, Cowgirl," Charlie would call out each time she arrived, jumping out of the car, and racing to the barn. All the things that Mindy had learned that summer…how to curry the horses, what to feed them, how to saddle and bridle them properly…she had learned from Charlie.

He was the one who was teaching her to ride. In the afternoons, after finishing work, they would saddle up and go off for a riding lesson.

Today, Mindy sat on the fence of the circular training corral and watched excitedly as Charlie began to train the new horse. The three year old had never been ridden, a green horse he called him…"but it's time for him to go to school," Charlie chuckled.

"This is a job that needs patience," Charlie walked over to her and explained. The horse's ears laid flat against his head as he eyed Charlie suspiciously. "First two steps…getting him use to me being up close and use to the sound of my voice."

Charlie walked slowly towards the three year old lineback Dun. When he was five feet away, the horse lowered his head shying away in fear of the man. "Easy boy," Charlie murmured. "I'm not going to hurt you." He walked toward the horse again.

The big animal jumped and bucked high in the air, and hit the ground running directly towards Mindy, perched on the fence. It seemed impossible a horse could move so quickly. Before Mindy could jump down, the brown streak crashed into the fence. Yanking her foot away, Mindy was relieved to find her leg in one piece, even though her boot was crushed between the horse and the fence.

"You OK, Cowgirl?" Charlie shouted, moving quickly to her side.

"I'm fine," she exclaimed breathlessly, "but my boot looks kind of smushed." They examined it together.

"No harm done that a good polishing won't cure," Charlie said. "And you learned a mighty important lesson too. A green horse is a very dangerous critter. You must always be ready to move out of his way, and move plenty fast! They may look calm, but remember, this is all new to him. When an animal feels fear, he's liable to do anything, and until we convince him we're friends, he will respond to us in fear."

Mindy nodded her head, and climbed back up on the fence. "I'm ready this time for a quick trip to the ground. I won't take my eyes off of him!"

"Good boy," Charlie said, as horse and Man eyed each other cautiously. Charlie talked softly and still the animal balked, but eventually, Charlie was able to walk up and stand close to the horse.

Talking to reassure him, he reached out to put his hand on the horse's shoulder. Every muscle in the colts body tensed up. Mindy could see his shoulders tremble, but the horse stood firm allowing Charlie to touch him as he gently whispered to him.

"Hey!" shouted a loud voice. Mindy turned and saw a man with a harsh face striding toward her. "You gonna baby that horse, or throw a saddle on him and get em broke?" Joe was a new wrangler on Grandpa's spread. To Mindy it seemed he was always trying to pick a fight. His loud voice sent the dun skittering away toward the barn.

"Well, Joe, you keep storming up like that and I'll never get this horse broke. You've probably figured out that you and I are never gonna' agree on breaking horses," Charlie responded patiently. "That's why you have your horses to work with and I have mine." Charlie's patient voice irritated Joe even more than if Charlie would have hollered back.

"We'll see who gets the job done first. Mr. Cunningham's owners want horses ready to work and ride, not to be pets." He stomped off leaving Charlie to shrug his shoulders.

"Now that is one hard man there," Charlie said. "I wonder what got him to be so dad gum cantankerous? Half the time he's yelling at me and the horses and the other half I catch him sneaking around the barn looking for who knows what. He's great with the horses, but he won't be here long. Your grandpa doesn't like the rough way he treats the horses he's training."

"Well, its probably about time to call it quits on the training for today" He opened the gate to the stall, and sure enough, the nervous dun trotted right in. "Let's head up to the house and see what Netta has for a snack."

***

The big lodge with its wide porch was an inviting place. There were rocking chairs for reading, or just sitting and enjoying the dozens of hummingbirds that came to drink the red sugar water in the hummingbird feeders. They seemed to stop, suspended in mid air looking for just the right spot to land and dip into the feeders. If a hummer had the perch wanted by another bird, the aerial battle would begin. They attacked each other, swooping and diving until each one was settled onto a spot.

Karilynn, Mindy's little sister, and Aunt Netta were just placing lemonade and a big plate of chocolate chip cookies on the porch table. "Aunt Netta let me help make the cookies and I think they're the best ever," Karilynn bragged. She plopped down in a rocker. She sat a large stuffed bear on her lap. On closer inspection, you might notice that the bear's mouth was covered with cookie crumbs and a smear of chocolate.

"I thought I could smell these all the way down at the barn," Charlie said with a twinkle in his eye. "Hmmm, these are mighty good cookies." He sat down and helped himself to another cookie and took a long draw of lemonade that Aunt Netta had poured into chilled mugs.

"I'm sure glad you girls were able to come over one more time before school starts," said Aunt Netta.

At the mention of school, Mindy's face clouded over.

"Mindy and Josh don't want to start a new school, but I do," Karilynn declared. She had never met anyone but a friend and loved being with people.

"Well, I sure don't," Mindy said back to Karilynn, sulking.

"You know, Mindy," Charlie said, "my old Pappy use to say that just as a horse needs training to do his work, kids need school so they can amount to something in this life. Of course, he never went to school himself, so I don't know if he had any clue what he was talking about!" Aunt Netta kicked Charlie under the table and raised her eyebrows in his direction.

"Um...well, what I mean is, just like you and I are starting to school that horse, Mindy, it will be a good thing for you three kids to start to school, too. You don't want to grow up ignorant and useless," Charlie completed his speech and looked over to Aunt Netta who smiled and nodded an approval.

Mindy nibbled around the edge of her cookie and said, "I just want to work around the ranch with horses like you do. I'll learn a lot more here than I would in some dumb old school."

***

At last, that dreaded first day of school dawned bright. The Colorado air was crisp and clear. Unlike Texas, where the Cunninghams were born and lived until their move to Colorado, the smell of fall already filled the air. Autumn never began in Texas until early November, so it was really hot when school started in August.

"It should be a gloomy day," Mindy complained. The children were sitting at the table and the air was filled with the smell of pancakes and bacon. Mother had made their favorite breakfast for the first day of school. Josh brushed aside a large bumble bee that had landed on his plate and looked to be eating its share of Josh's breakfast. Josh reached for another tall stack of pancakes and poured on the last of the hot syrup from the small silver pitcher. He seldom let his feelings interfere with eating his mom's cooking.

"I am willing to bet, Mindy, that before the week is out, you'll find something to make your face as bright as that sun." Mom nodded towards the early morning sunshine that was streaming through the kitchen windows.

"Well, it sure won't help matters to whine about it! We've all got to go and that's that!" Josh was resigned to his new school fate. He attacked his second stack of pancakes as if he hadn't eaten in weeks.

Mrs. Cunningham sighed and turned to the sink to begin the breakfast cleanup.

Karilynn got up and began to clear her and Mindy's empty plates from the table. "We've had so many adventures this summer since we've come to this old cabin, why can't we have some more at our new school?" Karilynn suggested as she slid back into her seat, her lips pursed as she considered the possibility.

The sun slid behind the clouds and darkened the room. "Whoooah!" All three heads swung around at the sound of BF's voice. There sat Karilynn's bear on the sideboard, staring at them with a gleam in his eyes. Karilynn quickly looked over to her mother to see if she had heard the voice, but she was loudly washing up the breakfast things! Karilynn's eyes returned to her bear's face and he winked at her.

"Oh my!" she said, and sent a warm smile his way. "It looks as if BF Bear and our Bees are hinting at another Cunningham family adventure," Karilynn giggled, as she watched the two bees excitedly circling the room looking for trouble.

"Well, at least one of my kids is happy to be going back to school." Mom said unknowingly. As she turned away from the sink her eyes caught sight of the two bees flying through her kitchen. She swatted at them with her tea towel and mumbled about getting the exterminator out.

With hands on her hips and bees on her mind, she instructed, "Now, one and all…be you happy or sad…it's time to face the adventure of a new school," she smiled encouragingly as she shooed the kids out the kitchen door.

CHAPTER 2

BULLIES, TEACHERS AND FRIENDS

"Here comes our bus," Karilynn said excitedly.

"Ready for the first day?" questioned Doc. He had dropped by to give them a ride to the bus stop and to give the kids a few off-to-school gifts. Doc was just tucking a new Winnie the Pooh spiral notebook into Karilynn's backpack as the bus pulled up. Josh had already slipped a cool notebook that was covered with motorcycles into his pack. Mindy was tracing her finger over the cover of hers…"Of course, I got horses for you, Cowgirl," Doc chuckled.

Josh watched Mindy try to make room for her notebook in her backpack. "You sure have lots of girly stuff in there," Josh smirked.

"There, it's all in," Mindy huffed, as she slung it on her back.

The sunny sky darkened as a few dreary clouds rolled across the sky. A gust of wind stirred up the dirt on the road. Mindy shivered, but not from the chilly air. "Doom and gloom approaches," she moaned.

"No, adventure comes!" Doc said encouragingly. He wanted to say more, but thought better of it, and instead gave each kid a quick hug and a shove toward the bus.

All three climbed up the steps of the yellow school bus and took empty seats near the middle. Only two other kids were on board. And if anyone was paying attention, they would have noticed one rather large insect boarding the bus and crawling into Josh's shirt pocket.

"Now that I have driven all the way out here for you five, I can get back to the main road and get the rest of the little monsters," complained the heavy-set bus driver.

"You just do that, Mr. Wooley," one of the boys answered from the back of the bus. "Baaaa, baaaa," he finished off his sentence with loud sheep noises.

"You start that stuff again this year, John, and I'm gonna' tape your mouth shut with duct tape."

"You really got me worried, Mr. Wooley," the boy sneered defiantly.

As the bus lurched forward and groaned it's way from first to second gear, the two boys swung towards the front and took two aisle seats across from the Cunningham kids.

"You guys must be new this year?" the boy named Herm asked brusquely.

"Yeah," answered Josh cautiously. His body stiffened as he guessed what the two mean looking boys had in mind.

"Well, I'm also new here this year, right John?"

"Yeah, Herm, but your Grandpa didn't have to put you on the bus. Aren't you three a little old to be babysat at the bus stop?" The two boys looked at each other and laughed.

Josh eyed the boys wearily. He had come up against boys just like these in his old school in Texas. Both John and Herm wore attitudes that shouted, "bullies."

"He's just a friend who brought us a gift for the first day of school," Karilynn answered in a friendly voice. Typical of Karilynn, everyone was a potential friend and she had failed to notice the wary look on Josh's face nor the mean attitude of the boys.

"By the way, what kind of name is Herm?" asked Josh innocently, with an elbow from Mindy. "Sounds like some kind of a disease."

Whap! Herm punched Josh hard on the shoulder. The bee buzzing around him just missed being squashed. Josh jumped up and pulled the boy out of his seat.

"Hey, I just saved you from being stung! What's your problem?" the boy smirked, pushing Josh back down in his seat. He boldly stood up again, this time joined by Mindy. Both boys looked back at them fearlessly.

"Get lost," Josh said, and nudged Mindy back into her seats. The boys laughed again and reclaimed their spots at the back of the bus.

"That's just great!" Josh's voice vibrated as they bounced over the washboard ruts in the road.

Karilynn climbed on her knees and leaned over into her brother and sister's seat. "They're mean," Karilynn said in a surprised voice. She grabbed hold of the bar on the back of her seat, as the bus bounced her around. Karilynn motioned for them to lean forward.

The Cunningham kids put their heads together. "I'm not scared, though," she said quietly. "Did you see the way BF Bear looked at us this morning when I talked about adventures? And Mr. Bee, riding on your shoulder, going to school with us!"

"I saw," Josh agreed. All three children had discovered over the summer that their Grandfather's cabin had some unusual visitors. There were several comings and goings of uninvited, though not unwelcomed guests. BF Bear and two huge bumble bees seemed to have moved in and claimed the cabin as their home. Things had been very quiet with the mysterious three-some for several months until just this morning.

Mindy who had been quiet, sighed. "Well, I'm glad that you're so anxious for this adventure, Karilynn. I know one thing. I don't want anything to do with those two brats! Let's stay as far away from them as possible. Sure not a very promising start to the new school year," she sighed again.

The bus took one final bounce, and rolled onto some smooth pavement. Mr. Wooley shifted into third gear, gathered up some speed, and lumbered down the blacktop highway. At each stop more and more kids climbed on. Most of the students ignored the Cunninghams, as they excitedly greeted old friends. But a few nodded and said a quick hello.

***

Life did not improve noticeably for Mindy as she slid into her first period pre-algebra class. Apparently, the teacher had already called her name a couple of times for attendance. "Uh, I'm here Ms. Shulkey," noticing the older teacher's name printed neatly on the blackboard.

"I expect all of my students to be here on time or suffer the consequences," barked Ms. Shulkey, over her coke-bottle glasses. "You've used up your one free late-to-class-pass. Don't let it happen again!"

"Yes ma'am, it won't happen again...*you ole' battleaxe*," Mindy mumbled under her breath in what she assumed was an unintelligible level.

"What was that young lady?" snapped Ms. Shulkey back at her.

Mindy's temper often took her to the edge of big trouble. She cleared her throat to try and cover her insolent words. "Ah, excuse me," she said locking eyes with the grumpy teacher.

When the bell rang Mindy was the first one out of the classroom. Even though one boy had laughed and given her a thumbs up, she was regretting getting on her teacher's bad side the very first day. It wouldn't pay and she knew it. Mindy walked slowly down the hall towards her next class, feeling miserable. "Hey, Mindy!" She turned around at the sound of her name.

Mindy's eyes widened in disbelief. Rushing towards her was her friend Shannon who she had met last summer in Colorado Springs. Both Josh and Mindy had stayed in Shannon's house for several days while Karilynn was in the hospital. She had a concussion and broken leg from a collision on a four-wheeler, which also involved an encounter with a bear.

"What are you doing here, Shannon?"

"Guess what!" she laughed, holding out her textbooks and a Monte Vista class schedule card. "I'm new in school here, just like you." Mindy couldn't believe her eyes and stood speechless in front of her friend. "My Dad has come to take over as president of one of the local banks. Our move has been up in the air for weeks, but I didn't want to call you until I knew for sure. I was afraid to get our hopes up," she smiled.

"I can't believe it," Mindy said. "Oops, I don't want to be late to my second class…I'll explain later," Mindy rushed on. "Let's talk at lunch…we can have lunch together, can't we?" Mindy's thoughts ran together with the excitement she was feeling. "I eat at noon."

"Me, too! Get going," Shannon said, as she gave her friend a push down the hall!

***

Josh sat on the bleachers listening to his PE teacher. This class should be fun. It sounded like they would play several different sports and football tryouts were coming up. Josh had lunch with two other boys who were new, and he was now sitting with a kid he had met in his history class. So far, all of his teachers seemed friendly enough.

The only crummy part of his day had been a hard push in the hall from John and Herm. "Thank goodness they're a year ahead of me and I don't have classes with them," he thought to himself. "I can find ways to steer clear…Oh no!" Josh gulped as he looked up and spotted the very same bullies entering the gym.

They sat down with the older boys at the end of the bleachers. "You're late again," the coach hollered to the two boys. "Give me six laps around the gym. John, you've been here long enough to know to be on time." Herm and John glared at the coach, and stomped off to the edge of the gym. "There is no reason to be late to my class," the coach explained. "You WILL be on time, and suited out every day for PE unless you have a signed excuse from the office. We are here to learn discipline, teamwork, and develop our personal skills in each sport."

Coach Tugboat Jones was living up to his reputation. Josh heard he had been nicknamed "Tugboat" in his college days due to his size and ability to play hard nosed football. Students, however, only called him Mr. Jones to his face, and had better not be caught calling him anything else.

The Coach taught PE as a serious class and expected a lot from the students. Josh loved sports and was confident that he would be athletic enough to win Tugboat's approval and stay on his good side. Josh smiled to himself. This was his last class and he had made it through his first day.

***

Karilynn walked happily alongside some other third graders, new friends who would be sitting with her on the bus. Except for the morning flap with those two bullies, her day had gone along as she had expected. A great new teacher and lots of new friends. She waved at Josh and Mindy who were in their seats toward the middle of the bus. She grabbed a seat no longer feeling like a stranger, but a welcomed newcomer.

***

Aunt Netta pushed through the swinging doors of the kitchen as she carried a tray full of warm biscuits and strong coffee that she had prepared for her brother. "This coffee is strong enough to stand on its own," she thought to herself, but she always prepared it just the way that Mr. Cunningham liked it!

"Those kids need a grandpa," she heard a loud voice booming out of Grandpa's office. "Why am I the one taking them to the bus stop this morning? Those kids need support as they face a new school in a new town," the voice said emphatically. "What's wrong with you helping out?"

"Oops," thought Aunt Netta. "I think I need another cup of coffee." She slid the tray onto the hall table and marched back to the kitchen.

"I'm not interested, Bob." Grandpa Daniel was sitting at his desk, while Doc stood in front of him, his fist doubled up at his side. Doc, Grandpa and Aunt Netta were playmates when they were young and had grown up together. That was a lot of years to be friends.

"I didn't ask for them to come, and I sure don't need any of Dan's pesky kids bothering me. I was no good raising him, and I won't be any better with them." The two old friends glared at each other. Neither one was going to back down.

"Good morning, Bob." Aunt Netta greeted Doc as she bustled into the room with a breakfast tray in hand. "You two old friends sit down and settle this over coffee and hot biscuits, with my fresh-made strawberry jelly. That should sweeten up both of your dispositions!"

"I thank you kindly for the offer," Doc said, "but I best be moving on to start my work which has been delayed long enough." He stomped out of the room and slammed the porch door as he let himself out of the lodge.

"He's right, you know, Daniel. You're missing out on…"

"Don't you start in on me, too, Netta," Daniel growled. "I've got enough chores waiting on me today to fill up a week." And with that, the second grouch marched out the door. Aunt Netta sighed, picked up a biscuit and her cup of coffee and went out to sit on the front porch before her day's work began.

CHAPTER 3

NEW SCHOOL SURPRISES

Two weeks of school had passed. For Mindy it was like a roller coaster ride. Some days were up and other days seemed like a race to the bottom. Her stomach churned each time she went to the new school. She was so relieved to have Shannon as a friend, she was forgetting to be sociable to the other girls. She handled the schoolwork fine, but her teachers seemed to be on the lookout for that stubborn outspoken girl they'd heard about.

Josh was finding his place with the other boys who were into sports. His schoolwork was easy enough, but the hard work was keeping away from the bullies.

Karilynn's friendly personality helped her make a smooth entrance into the third grade where everyone seemed to consider her their new best friend.

On the third Monday, all the students were told to report to the school auditorium. Mindy and Josh filed in with the other students, each looking for a friend to sit with. Mindy slipped in beside Shannon near the front, while Josh saw his new friends horsing around towards the back of the room.

"What is this all about, Mindy?" whispered Shannon.

"I don't know, but here comes Mr. Noble." The principal, a bald man with a well-trimmed white beard and very rosy cheeks, stepped up to the podium motioning for the students to find their seats. His jolly face had earned him the nickname, The Noble Santa.

"Attention, students, attention. Find your places and sit down. We have a lot to cover this morning and we need to get started." Everyone began to quiet down as the principal's jovial voice boomed over the microphone.

Every assembly started out with the Pledge of Allegiance. This morning the Pledge was followed by a tall blond girl with a squeaky soprano voice singing the National Anthem.

"Thank you, Darlene, for opening our assembly this morning," he nodded with a smile. Now on to business." Mr. Noble cleared his throat loudly and straightened his tie. "We are here today to talk about our second annual *Outdoor School.*" Mr. Noble grinned widely, all 125 of his teeth showing. An excited hum could be heard around the auditorium as the students responded to this announcement.

"We had a great time last year, didn't we?…well, didn't we?" Mr. Noble cupped his hand to his ear when he didn't get the response he wanted.

"Yeeeaaaa," the kids yelled and clapped their hands. When Mr. Noble was in a jolly mood, the students knew they should respond in kind.

"I had a great time last year," said Jeff, Josh's new friend. "You get out of school for three days. What could be better than that?"

Mindy and Shannon just looked at each other with puzzled expressions wondering what *Outdoor School* was all about. Mindy pictured kids lugging heavy desks outside to the playground to have classes.

"I've entitled this year's *Outdoor School, Understanding Monte Vista's Role in Colorado's History.*" Pleased with himself, he patted his stomach like a satisfied bear with a tummy full of honey. "And now I want to introduce you to some special guests we're adding to our staff just for this year's *Outdoor School.* Several men walked onto the stage and sat down in empty chairs that had been placed there for them.

"First of all, we have Mr. Smoklin, our local forest ranger from the National Forest Service. Mr. Smoklin stood and nodded to the audience. He's in charge of the 5th and 6th grade *Environmental Research Quest.*

"Now that sounds boring," whispered a fifth grader sitting in front of Mindy and Shannon to her friend.

"No kidding!" was the girl's reply.

"This will be an exciting quest that will start at the Grizzly Lake Trailhead and take you 5th and 6th graders up to the high mountain lakes to study the cycle of our rivers, the fish of high lakes and animals native to our area.

The girl in front turned and gave her friend a big yawn.

"As you may know," Mr. Noble said, with a twinkle in his eyes, "Grizzly Lake is too far to go on foot and so we are providing each student with a veteran trail horse." The student's faces lit up and excited whispers could be heard around the room.

"And now," Mr. Noble said as he held up his hand for quiet, "I want you to meet Mr. Charlie Summers, who will be in charge of teaching you to saddle and pack your horses and how to ride the trails."

Mindy could not believe her eyes when *her* Charlie stood up and waved. He had on dark jeans that had been pressed, a white shirt and bolo tie, with a new brown felt Stetson hat.

No wonder Mindy had not recognized him. She had never seen him so dressed up! Charlie looked her right in the face and gave her a wink. She returned the wink with a big smile.

"Now for you 7th and 8th graders, I want to introduce you to Dr. Bob Stephens. Doc Stevens, as he is known around here, is an expert on local mining and railroad history. He will be leading *The Industrial Quest* to understand what role these huge industries have played in the settlement of our valley."

"Dr. Stephens has received many awards, both from the private sector and from the government for his vital research in the area of inter-stellar mining, which you will learn more about this week. We are so grateful to you, Dr. Stephens, for coming along with us on the exploration of our own history!" Josh and Mindy both sat with their mouths open as Mr. Noble introduced Doc. He stood and saluted the crowd of kids.

"Oh, I mustn't forget to introduce his constant companion, who will be going along, Killer." Mr. Noble waved a hand in Doc's direction, and sure enough, there was their favorite big black dog sitting at attention behind Doc's chair. All the students laughed and applauded. Killer did not twitch, but sat obediently beside Doc looking out at the kids.

"Also, you third and fourth graders are in for a big treat. During the day you will be learning to use a compass and hike with a typography map. In the evenings, you will explore the night sky observing constellations and learning the characteristics of stars. Your *Quest to the Heavens* will be led by our third grade teacher, Mrs. June Hines and our elementary school science teacher, Mr. Henry Utter. You will camp in the nearby minor's ghost town of Iron City."

Karilynn was pleased that her teacher had been chosen to lead her group. But the thought of a ghost town did make her a little nervous.

"*Outdoor School* will begin next week. Ranger Smoklin will be making special presentations before we go, explaining camping safety and how to treat our forest with respect. A part of his presentation will include fire safety for our forest, so expect to see Mr. Smoklin in your classes. When we return from our *Outdoors School*, we don't want to leave a single sign of our visit."

"Coach Jones will be passing out your study notebooks for the trip. Please note that there is a waiver in your notebook that your parents must sign for you to go on this excursion. No waiver, no cool trip." With that, Mr. Noble dismissed them with a wave and his usual kind words…"Now off to class with you, my favorite students!"

***

The bus ride home that afternoon had been full of excited students making plans for their part of the Outdoor School. "At least that keeps them from pestering me," Mr. Wooly mumbled under his breath. Both Herm and John had been absent from school today, and that made his life easier, because they were always rowdy and picking on the other kids. "Never let it be said that I'm not thankful for small things."

Finally the bus turned onto the familiar dirt road and began its creaky assent up the valley. At their stop, the three Cunningham kids hopped off. Karilynn turned to give Mr. Wooly a big smile and a wave goodbye. She was determined to win him over, but so far she was finding it to be a very difficult task.

"What the heck are they doing here," Josh hollered, unable to believe his eyes. There in the middle of the deer path that weaved down to their cabin, stood a huge moose with two giant bumblebees perched on his sizeable, flat, horns. Their dog, Hank Williams Jr...or Hank for short... completed the unusual gathering.

The huge moose stood firmly planted across their path. It was as if he was saying, "Don't pass this way." The bees began flying a crisscross pattern in front of the children's faces and then flying off down a different trail. Hank took off after the bees, and then stopped, looking back over his shoulder at the kids, barking and leaping into the air.

Most kids would be quite surprised to find this kind of a greeting party waiting to meet them. However, Karilynn, Mindy, and Josh had already found themselves tangled in numerous adventures with these strange critters over the past summer.

"I wonder what's going on?" asked Mindy, chewing on her bottom lip.

"Fifty Point seems to be blocking our way home, and Mr. and Ms. Bee, and Hank want us to follow them," Karilynn explained the obvious, pointing in the direction of the excited critters.

"Yeah, I can see that, Karilynn," Josh muttered mockingly. He was tired from school and wanted to get home. "What do you think, Mindy?"

"I think that if we don't get on home, Mom will have The Cavalry out looking for us," Mindy sighed. She then started toward the old deer path leading to their cabin. The moose ambled forward and met her face-to-face. He gave her a gentle nudge with his muzzle back towards the others.

"Hey, watch it!" Mindy exclaimed. She again tried to walk around Fifty Points. "Brruummph," he bellowed as he pushed her again, harder and she tripped and landed on the ground.

Hank ran over and licked her face, whining, as if to say, "Come on this other way!" He ran back down the trail where the bees were hovering in the air.

"Oooooh, I'm so not in the mood for games like this," Mindy said in frustration as she jumped up and brushed the dirt off of her jeans.

They looked in the direction of Fifty Point, who had planted his hoofs in a wide determined stance.

"It doesn't look like we're going that way," Josh commented.

"Obviously not," Karilynn said. "Look, they want us to go this other way for some reason, so let's just do it!" Karilynn often forgot she was the youngest. When her practical mind saw something clearly, she did not hesitate to order the others around.

After a brief chat, the kids started following along behind the noisy bees. "We'll go with you, but we need to do it in a hurry and get on home," Mindy spoke, shaking her finger at both bees and the dog. The moose brought up the rear as if to discourage anyone who might turn back.

When Hank saw the children following, he barked a command and the bees flew off down the trail. Hank ran along behind. Soon their pace had changed to a jog in order to keep up with the bees and Hank.

The trail wound up a steep hill, and each child had to slow down. After awhile, Josh, who was in front, stopped. "I gotta catch my breath." He was doubled over taking in deep breaths of air. Karilynn and Mindy were grateful for the rest and threw their packs on the ground. The animals surrounded them, looking on patiently. Allowing a three-minute rest, Hank then darted up the trail barking insistently to get the children to move on. The moose gently nuzzled each kid, and the bees buzzed as if to say, "We need to get going!"

"Do you smell something," Josh asked, as he rose to his feet.

"What now?" whined Mindy, getting up with a groan. "Oh, I do smell something burning," she exclaimed. The three children looked at each other and, with renewed energy raced up the hill to where Hank stood.

"Oh no," Karilynn yelled and pointed. "Look down there!"

The children looked down from their vantage point on the high hill. They could plainly see a thick cloud of gray smoke coming up from the floor of the forest below. Even though the children had never actually seen a forest fire before, it was the first thought that jumped into their minds.

"Maybe it's a campfire?" Mindy asked hopefully.

"Not that big," Josh answered, slightly bent forward trying to catch his breath. "But I was reading in the Monte Vista News that the Forest Service was conducting controlled fires to clean out parts of the forest. Maybe that's what we're seeing."

Karilynn had remained quiet, but she kept looking down at the smoke and back to their animal friends. They were silent as if to let the children process the sight on their own.

Karilynn noticed the fur on Hank's neck standing on end as the bees waited expectantly, perched on the moose's horns. The big animal quivered with excitement standing ready to act. "I don't think our four friends would have gone to all this trouble to bring us here if something wasn't up!"

Josh frowned at his little sister and sighed, "a heavy duty thinker in my pee wee sister's body. But I honestly think you're right!"

"OK, so now what?" Mindy directed her question to the waiting animals.

"Brruummph, home!" The moose grumbled and began to lumber down the other side of the hill!"

While down on the forest floor, as if to reinforce the need to hurry, another pinion burst into bright flames. All three saw the horrifying display of color and took off to follow Fifty Point running at top speed. The children were in an unfamiliar part of the woods, but set their confidence in their forest friends that were herding them toward their home territory and safety.

CHAPTER 4

FIRE

Moose, bees, dog and children arrived at their cabin in less time than the kids thought possible. "Mom, Mom," Josh, the first to arrive, shouted as he ran into the kitchen. Mrs. Cunningham looked up from the stove where she was taking hot sugar cookies from her oven.

"What's going on," she began to ask, but Josh broke in with a breathless holler.

"Forest fire…over there," he tried to explain while pointing back to the forest, but his mouth would not co-ordinate with his words.

Mindy burst in the door and said, "We spotted a forest fire down below Lincoln Ridge. It's just beginning, Mom…hurry up and call Mr. Smoklin…or Doc. Just do something," she pleaded.

"You're sure it's a fire?" Mom questioned, still not able to take them quite seriously, but moving towards the phone none-the-less.

"Very sure," Mindy said, and Karilynn and Josh both nodded their heads in agreement.

She quickly dialed The National Forest Service office and asked to speak to Mr. Smoklin. Trying to explain what she'd just heard, she looked at the children with confusion stamped on her face.

"Here, I'll explain," said Josh who found himself now able to breathe and talk at the same time. He quickly described what they had seen at Lincoln Ridge. "Could it be a controlled burn, sir?"

"I know where those burns are scheduled right now, and none are scheduled in that area."

"It was too big to be a campfire," Josh exclaimed. I know it's hard to believe, but…"

"I trust you, Josh. Don't worry! I'll hang up and get the wheels rolling to get it checked out. I'll be back in touch," the forest ranger assured Josh as he hung up.

"Sit," said Mom, "and I'll get you three something to drink and some hot cookies." The children did as they were told, glad to be receiving something to quench their thirst. Suddenly they felt exhausted now that they had made their report and knew that help was on the way. The adrenaline that pushed them home had left them drained of any energy.

"Forest Fires are a bad thing," Karilynn said with tears in her eyes. "If they get out of hand, they can burn lots and lots of trees. And lots of animals can be pushed out of their homes, or even die!" Her sensitive heart pushed a tear out of her eye, and it trickled down her cheek. The bear in her lap made a comforting growling sound.

"People's houses go, too," Josh retorted. "I hope it won't come this way."

"Well, we've done all we can do right now," Mother said as she sat down glasses of cold lemonade. She returned again to the table with a big plate of warm sugar cookies fresh out of the oven. "Now we have to wait and see!"

"Pisst!" Mindy caught Josh and Karilyn's attention and nodded toward the window. All three kids could see two large figures standing at the edge of their woods.

"Thanks for the snack, Mom" Mindy said as she slid her chair away from the table.

"Where are you going, kids? I don't want you exploring the fire. I want you to stay right here with me until we see what's what."

Josh gulped down his last swig of lemonade. "We're just gonna hang out in front and see if we can see any smoke." The three kids headed out the door towards the two large animals who had stepped back into the woods, so as not to arouse their mom's suspicions.

"I don't see or smell anything," Mom reported as she joined the kids outside but stopped on the porch. She stood for a few minutes, hands on her hips, a worried look on her face.

"We'll keep watch, Mom, don't worry," Mindy encouraged her. Satisfied she turned and walked back into the kitchen.

Assured of being left alone, they rushed into the tall trees. Waiting there by the dilapidated log fence, were the two large moose. The children never felt quite safe around this moose couple. But in their past summer adventure, the animals had shown their allegiance to them.

The female moose brumbled nosily, and nuzzled Fifty Point's neck to call the kids' attention to him. It had been an unnecessary gesture.

The children's eyes had already wandered over to the male moose and they wrestled with their desire to laugh out loud.

There he stood decked out with school bags, and sweatshirts draped around his big head and his large, flat antlers. A Dallas Cowboy cap hung by its strap from his left horn.

Everyone knows this rule---When you are trying not to laugh don't look at each other! Karilynn, Mindy and Josh with wide eyes stared straight ahead, sensing that Fifty Point did not like being used as a pack animal. His bossy mate, who was not equipped with horns to do what she had considered an important job, had coaxed him into it. To laugh would make matters worse for him.

Josh stepped forward. Before he could speak, Ms. Manners brumbled again, and said sternly, "Here are your things! You left them in the woods. Not at all like responsible children. You should learn to keep them out of the elements!"

"Now, Manners," scolded BF Bear, who Karilynn had dragged along to join in the Moose Meeting. "There was the immediate need of reporting the fire!!"

"An important item, of course," Manners agreed, "but what if these school books had been rained on...ruined, they would have been ruined!"

"We're in a drought," Mindy muttered under her breath angrily.

Missing the words, Ms. Moose admonished Mindy. "Mannerly young ladies *do not mutter*!" It was good, very good that the Moose had not heard Mindy's sarcastic reply. "Now gather up your things. You will not miss a single day of homework due to the fact that we saved your books from who-knows-what."

Josh opened his mouth to complain but she butted in. "Brruummph! No need to thank us, Josh, just go in and start on your lessons."

"Just a minute, Manners," said BF Bear. He seemed to be the only one around who could speak up to the Moose. "We need to talk about The Fire before they go in." Manners eyed him with a cold stare, and sauntered away from the group.

"Yes, please," said Karilynn. "We have so many questions!"

"Thanks for bringing our things back, Fifty Point," said Josh as he stood on his tiptoes and reached to retrieve their belongings.

He wanted to get the moose out of his misery, and indeed the moose looked greatly relieved to have his neck and horns out from under the decorations of school bags and clothes.

The children spent the next few minutes asking questions about the fire. BF and Fifty Point answered them all because, of course, they know all there is to know about Forest Fires.

"Wind. It all depends on the wind. Firefighters can contain fire, if the wind lets them," summarized the moose who spoke few words for obvious reasons.

"We'll have to wait and hear from Mr. Smoklin. Fire in the forest is considered an emergency of the worst kind, and the Forest Service is quick to respond. We'll know soon," BF Bear said.

The Moose called an end to the meeting as he dipped his head politely to the group and sauntered off into the forest. "Don't let all of this excitement make you forget your lessons," Ms. Moose grumbled as she joined her mate on the trail.

***

Arriving at the front door of the cabin, the children pushed past the screen door into the kitchen. "Oh, you've got your school things," Mother said. I wondered what had happened to your book bags." Mrs. Cunningham's way was to cook, cook, cook whenever there was stress lurking in the air. In the short time since they had arrived home and reported the fire, the sweet smell of sugar cookies had been replaced by sweet potato french fries sizzling in one pan, while the aroma of chicken Piccata poured out of the oven door. Other unidentified food bubbled on the stove, promising a meal that would be too big for one family. "Where did you leave them?"

"We left them in the forest, but they were returned to us… by…uh…by Moose Express," Karilynn, who was always truthful, mumbled.

"Moose Express?" asked Mom with a puzzled look. Fortunately for the kids, a loud stomping of boots on the front porch shifted Mom's thoughts towards the kitchen door. Doc Stephens and his dog Killer appeared at the entry.

"Come on in, Doc," Mrs. Cunningham said with a welcoming smile. With Mr. Cunningham gone from home so much, she had learned to lean on this wise and sensible man. "Do you have any news of the fire? Do we have reason to think it might come our way?" She automatically set down a plate of cookies before him.

Doc's face was lined with worry. His bushy eyebrows seemed wilder than ever, and the sparkle of his blue eyes had faded to a worried gray. Killer, who rarely left Doc's side, sat at attention on the front porch with his ears perked up. Even Hanks playful attacks did not distract his watchful eye.

"Right now, it seems that it won't come our way," Doc said. "The wind has kicked up as you can hear." It was true. The early autumn wind was whistling loudly through the pines.

"Wind in the forest, burns black scars in our hearts," BF bear quoted from an old American Indian Proverb, speaking softly so only the children could hear him. Nevertheless, Josh gave him a silencing glance. BF put his paw over his mouth.

"It was good thinking by you children to get the word out before the fire spread, but unfortunately the wind has already escalated the flames. It's moving towards Gold Camp road now, and they have called out all the area fire fighters from miles around."

"Won't all of those men be able to stop it?" Karilynn asked, mouth agape.

"I don't know, darling," Doc said with a sigh. "Our five-year drought is an enemy to the forest, and an ally for the fire. It's awfully dry out there!"

Suddenly, Killer's sharp, loud bark broke into their conversation.

"What's the matter, ol' boy?" Doc asked, walking to the door. Killer shot off the porch racing towards two boys stumbling out of the woods.

"Get away from me," demanded a boy who was kicking at the dog.

"Hey, mister, call your dog off!" shouted a worried voice in Doc's direction as he stepped out onto the porch.

Killer had backed the boys up against the barn wall, and imprisoned them by placing himself in the path of their escape. With each move they made, he growled a warning that halted their attempts to leave. Hank had joined in the barking and lunged in their direction.

Doc, Mindy and Josh hurried towards the barn, while Mom and Karilynn watched from the porch.

"Call your dog off, mister," Herm ordered in a nervous voice.

"Down King," Doc called the dog to his side. Killer obeyed and took his place by Doc, but his eyes remained glued on the boys. A low growl and ears flattened to his head brought the boys little comfort that they were out of danger.

"Call him off and let us go, mister," John demanded boldly, now that the dog was a few feet away. "If you don't, I'm gonna' tell my dad about your vicious dog. He's a County Commissioner and he'll take care of you and your dog!"

"What are you boys up to?" Doc inquired. He was puzzled by Killer's behavior. Usually when he sensed that Doc was in control, he would back off.

"Nothing. There's no law against hiking in the woods, is there?" Herm asked defiantly.

"I live over that way," John gestured in a general direction. "We were hiking to…uh…" he halted in mid-sentence, "over to…uhh…get ready for the Outdoor School that's coming up!" John seemed relieved with the lie that had popped into his head.

"Yeah, what's wrong with getting a start on our schoolwork?" Herm looked at them, eyes flashing angrily. "And Josh, ol buddy, with the 7th and 8th grades working together, me and John are planning some good times for you!"

"Outdoor School, eh?" Doc smiled at the boys mischievously. "So you two innocents will be in my group? I'm overjoyed to meet you ahead of time," Doc chuckled. Herm and John stood aghast as Doc explained that he would be the leader of the 7th and 8th grade group.

"And Killer's going, too," Josh explained with a grin. "He sure seems to have taken a liking for you two."

"Can't go far without my dog," Doc rubbed Killer's head. The dog did not change positions but remained on alert. "He is good protection against snakes, coyotes, and all kind of varmints," Doc explained, looking knowingly into the boy's eyes.

"He killed a bear once," Josh added enthusiastically.

"You kids, go on home," Doc said. "There's a forest fire, over toward Lincoln Ridge. This is no time for you to be wandering around in the woods."

"Forest fire?" repeated Herm. The boys exchanged anxious glances.

"Get on home," Doc said to the nervous boys. Without further encouragement, the boys ran off into the forest, looking back only to make sure that Killer wasn't following them.

Doc accepted an invitation for dinner. The widower enjoyed Mrs. Cunningham's cooking and there was plenty of food and plenty of talk around the table.

"Killer killed a bear?" Mindy asked Josh. "What do you mean he killed a bear?"

"Well… Josh got a little carried away out there," Doc grinned. "But I do wonder what those two scallywags were really up to?"

"If I know them," Josh said, "it was nothing good!"

CHAPTER 5

OUTDOOR SCHOOL

FALL OUTDOOR SCHOOL CHECKLIST	
Large Backpack	All Weather-Warm Clothes
Warm Sleeping Bag	Gloves
Pillow	Flashlight
Pocketknife	Maps (provided)
Binoculars	Compass
Study Diary	Energy bars
Warm hat/cap	Snacks for trail

Forget your textbooks; but don't forget your toothbrush

"That seems like an easy enough list," Mom said as she looked over the handout her kids had brought home describing the Outdoor School. "I thought they would cancel it with the forest fire burning out of control."

Mindy's forehead wrinkled up with alarm when she saw the four-days worth of cooking Mom had done in just one afternoon. "She's worried," Mindy thought. "Stacks of food, yep, she's worried!"

"We're going to be in a totally different area, Mom, not even close to the fire," Mindy said. She shuddered at the thought of Mom not letting them go. Boring things were planned at school for the children that chose to remain behind and not face the outdoor challenge. Mindy wanted no part of that.

"Toothbrush, no textbooks!" Josh's eyes lit up at the thought. "I'll make that trade any day."

"I can't wait for this new adventure," Karilynn twirled around the kitchen with excitement. She shared her Mom's view of making everything into an adventure. "But I'm glad that we don't have to do Survival Training until seventh grade. I don't want to stay alone in the woods for a whole night."

"Me either," exclaimed Mindy. "Even if I do have a horse to keep me company."

"Well, I'm not scared," boasted Josh. "Doc's survival training will have me ready. What's there to be afraid of anyway?"

"I don't know and I don't want to know," Mindy said.

"Lets see….wild animals, old Indian Spirits, dead minor's ghosts…" Karilynn counted off on her fingers with a worried frown.

"Yeah, and maybe one of them will sneak up on you while you're sleeping," Josh said maliciously. Plans began formulating in his mind.

"Stop it, Josh. I know you wouldn't be that mean to your sisters," exhorted mom. Josh flashed the girls a wicked grin. "And, the fire? The school wouldn't put you in any danger," Mom said firmly as if to convince herself.

Just then they heard the crunching of tires outside and a car door slam. "Open the door, Josh," Doc called out! He stepped through the door, loaded down with three large backpacks. "Your Dad called me to help you get your camping gear together. Josh, go get the sleeping bags out of my Jeep."

"I miss Dad so much." Karilynn's shining eyes filled up with tears.

"And he misses you guys, too. He wanted to take you shopping to get gear for the Outdoor School himself. However, when he found out he would not be back in time, he told me to buy you top of the line North Face camping gear. So, here it is."

The children had been surprised when they talked to their dad over the weekend. "I love to camp," he exclaimed when he learned about the Outdoor School Experience. "I guess any kid that grows up in Colorado gets the camping bug!"

Dad had grown up right down the road at Grandpa's ranch. He promised the kids he would show them his favorite places to camp out soon. "You won't find any tourist in my secret spots. These campsites are so far back in the woods, only crafty Indians and I can find them."

Finally the morning of Outdoor School arrived. The air was fresh and crisp under the brightest of Colorado skies. Many happy faces reflected the excitement of the outdoor adventure.

The students hung around in their groups laughing and talking, impatient to be on their way. Mindy repacked her gear, and Josh dipped into his mom's idea of trail mix.

Each Cunningham kid had crackers, cookies, cupcakes, cheese, cut up veggies, and a big bag of trail mix. Mom's recipe included nuts, seeds, raisins, chocolate chips and other unidentifiable bits and pieces that she promised would keep them energized for their adventure. She reluctantly handed each child four foiled wrapped energy bars. "I don't put much stock in these store-bought snacks.

They promise a lot, but who knows what's in them, probably old El Gato himself," she said sternly.

The strong odor of diesel, announced the arrival of the yellow school buses. They lumbered into the parking lot, and rolled to a stop with the whishing noise of brakes and the backfire of tired old engines.

Karilynn's group was the first to board a bus. Looking over her shoulder, she waved an excited good-bye to Josh and Mindy. All they saw was her waving hand, the majority of her body hidden by the backpack that was as big as she was.

Josh and his friend Jeff, pushed by Mindy and Shannon to find their bus. "Keep an eye out for spirits and ghosts," Josh said with a wicked grin.

"Yeah, see you girls real soon," Jeff mocked, joining in on Josh's threat.

"The boys climbed aboard their bus. Doc was counting noses and when he decided all were aboard, he gave the bus driver the signal to start her up.

"Look, that has to be our bus over there," Shannon said ignoring the boys' teasing. Two large horse trailers were parked by the bus where Shannon was pointing. The whole class of girls ran over, peeking into the trailers anxious to make friends. The boys sauntered over, curiosity written all over their faces.

"Load em up, Charlie" Mr. Smoklin said. "We'll assign horses first thing when we arrive at the trailhead. Until then it's Mr. Bixby's job to get us there."

***

An hour outside of town, the 7th and 8th grade bus turned up a rutted narrow road. "Jeff, how are we going to get up that steep road?" Josh's eyes opened wide when the old bus creaked and groaned, but continued on. The view off the right side of the bus was scary---a drop-off that fell straight down to the river below.

The girls let out oohs and aahs while the boys joked to cover their nervousness.

As they rounded a corner, Jeff gripped the window. "Look at that?" Josh's eyes followed where Jeff was pointing and gasped.

About a half a mile ahead you could see a large old wooden structure tilted out precariously over the road. "Are we going to drive under that?" one of the girls asked.

"Yep, we are, and you'd better hope the wind doesn't blow. It'll come down right on your side of the bus," piped up Herm, loud enough for the whole bus to hear. He and Germ seemed unshaken by the risky journey in the bus.

"Don't worry, we're almost there," Doc spoke up, glaring at the two boys. "Barnebus Busman knows these roads like the back of his hand, an expert actually. He flew F86 jets in the Korean war, so this bus is nothing to him," chuckled Doc.

The boys and girls looked at Mr. Busman, and didn't know whether to laugh or cry. He looked ancient in his wrinkled uniform, old hat, and thick glasses.

"Well, there's a big comfort," said one of the girls.

"It doesn't feel like a safe bet to me either," snickered her friend.

Jeff and Josh just looked at the two girls and shrugged their shoulders.

Five minutes later, as each kid held their breath, the driver downshifted and slowly rolled under the building hanging out over the road. There was a collective sigh as Barney pulled the bus away from the drop off and slowed to a stop.

The doors whished open and out jumped the kids. "Solid ground," thought Josh. Each kid watched astonished as Mr. Busman slowly turned the bus around on a slightly wider spot in the road, and began the slow lumber back down the mountain.

"OK guys, grab your gear. We've got a 30 minute hike up to the Molly Murphy Mine where we'll be setting up camp," barked Doc, before the kids could wander off. "Herm, you and John grab one of the coolers once you get your backpacks on, seeing how you've done all this before and are such big tough outdoorsmen." Both boys grumbled all the way up to the mine.

***

Meanwhile over at the Grizzly Lake trailhead, Charlie Summers, Mr.Smoklin, Mindy and Shannon had the 5th and 6th graders mounted up and ready to ride the high country. Mindy had her favorite horse, Lady, saddled up and Shannon was adjusting the stirrups on Butternut.

"Time to move em out guys," grinned Charlie as he rode by on Wrangler, his pride and joy from his rodeo days.

***

Sundown found nineteen tired kids gathered around the fire at the campsite near the Molly Murphy Mine, finishing up their burgers and lemonade. "Best meal I've ever had," announced Jeff tiredly, as he shoved down his second burger without missing a lick.

"Ok campers, time to get your tents set up and gear stowed away before it gets too dark to see," announced Coach Jones gruffly. He demonstrated by putting up his own tent as an example to those who had never put a tent up before. "Be sure and keep all foodstuffs out of your tents while you sleep or we'll have bears as overnight guests."

Just before turning in, Tugboat (aka Coach Jones), introduced Doc more formally to the 7th and 8th graders. "Dr. Stevens is an expert on the Molly Murphy gold mine and railroad history of our area. He will be leading your quest to understand what part the railroad and the old mine played in the settling of the area around Monte Vista. Gold was discovered in 1875 and forever changed the history of these mountains. Over 60 million dollars in gold was extracted over the next 40 years.

***

Meanwhile across the valley, Mr. Smoklin said, "Hit the sack students," as he finished outlining the next day's schedule of the Environmental Research Quest. "This quest will start at Grizzly Lake first thing in the morning. From there I'll lead you 5th and 6th graders up to the high mountain lakes to study the cycle of runoff streams, the fish of high lakes and the wild animals native to our area."

"Bruummmph", snorted Fifty Point, as the kids headed off to bed. "They should let us moose teach the kids about the wild animals native to this area since we know them first hand." Fifty Point just snuckeled (Moose snorting and chuckling) as he peered through the trees at the kids moving into their tents. "I'll take first watch," he announced, as Manners yawned and awkwardly curled up at his hoofs in the tall grass.

***

Way too early the next morning, Coach Jones blew his whistle shrilly to wake the 7th and 8th graders who would have sworn they had just gone to sleep a few minutes before. "Ok, kiddos, biscuits and bacon at the campfire in ten," Tugboat growled, as if he were still in the marines. "Mr. Smoklin's waiting on you guys, been up for hours you know."

By eight o'clock, Doc had the students outfitted for their adventures in the Molly Murphy Mine. Headlamps, day packs and specimen sacks made up their rucksacks. "Everybody is assigned a partner and you stay with them no matter what.

"Wouldn't you just know it, I've got Herm for my tunnel partner," mumbled Josh as Jeff glared at Germ who had been assigned to him. "What a way to ruin a good trip," making sure Herm and Germ heard his comments.

"You guys are gonna get your butts kicked if you keep your mouths flapping like that," snarled Herm as they headed nervously into the old mine with their helmet lights shining off the wet mossy walls.

"Hey, I got an idea," whispered Josh to Jeff, as they entered the mine….never dreaming of the untold trouble he was walking the two of them into. "According to my map, there's a shallow drop off up about a quarter of mile into the mine. Lets see if we can get those two nitwits to step over the edge."

"Isn't that a little risky?" asked Jeff nervously, as the class started spreading out in the narrow tunnels. "Nah, I got it all figured out," whispered Josh, a tad arrogantly. "Piece of cake, just hang back and we'll set em up."

Forty agonizing minutes later, found all four boys down at the bottom of an old landslide. Jeff and Josh had no working flashlights, no classmates within shouting distance and two enraged enemies ready to do some serious physical damage.

***

Meanwhile up at Grizzley Lake, Charlie had his group of 5th and 6th graders unsaddling their horses and setting up their base camp. Mindy and Shannon were great wranglers and Charlie didn't have a lot to do. "Lets get our camp set up and we'll grab a bite before we start poop, er….scat gathering."

"Before we do what?" asked a tow headed kid about the size of a large squirrel.

"Bruummmph," snuckeled Manners as the two moose peeked through the woods at the kids setting up camp. "Those kids look rather hopeless as future caretakers of our forest and streams."

"All kids look clueless at their age," responded Fifty Point, remembering their own kiddos as they stumbled about in their youth.

About that time, Mindy, having spotted her two friends in the woods, sneaked up on the two moose and gave a growl. Neither moose moved an inch as Manners commented, "You really think you can sneak up on a moose in the forest? We heard you coming a mile away…make that two miles away."

CHAPTER 6

ADVENTURE FIRE-OUT

Outdoor School behind them, school settled down to…well…
school, pretty much the way it was in Texas. Karilynn loved it
all. She especially loved school because she had won the award for
the best research project during Outdoor School. She'd got her
picture in the Monte Vista Mountain Bugle and won a cash prize
of $100 from the Chamber of Commerce. Karilynn, of course,
took all her friends out for burgers and fries at Jack's Burger Bar
in town.

Josh thought that school was a necessary evil; because without
school, there would be no sports! And sports were all that was
keeping him from heading back to Texas after Outdoor School.
If it wouldn't have been for Killer, Doc's dog, he might not be
playing sports at all. After having lured Herm and Germ into an
old abandoned mine shaft, he came within a hair of having been

stomped on by the big bullies. Fortunately, Killer had shown up at the last moment and rescued the boys and led them safely out of the mine. He'd even bitten ol' Germ on the butt.

And Mindy survived school by hanging out with Shannon in town, or at Grandpa's ranch with Charlie. She and Shannon had had a rather interesting Outdoor School memory involving poop...er... Scat. Knowing the boys planned on sneaking into their camp at night to do mischief, they'd preempted them by sneaking into the 7th and 8th grade campsite and leaving a few choice chunks of scat in certain bedrolls. The older kids were promising to get even.

But the really extraordinary thing that was affecting the school and indeed affecting the whole town...The Lincoln Ridge Fire! The flames, driven at the whim of the winds, spread the fire further and further up Chalk Creek and on over towards Cotton Wood Creek. It continued to blaze and spread, eating up hundreds of acres of forest.

Hundreds of fire fighters arrived daily from throughout the country to fight the tree eating flames. It was dangerous work for all involved as the fire spread rapidly.

***

Many days when the wind was from the west, even Monte Vista filled up with dark, gray smoke. Ashes fell like blackened snowflakes.

On these days the whole town was threatened by the live embers that could land anywhere. When embers landed in the wrong place... a stack of papers, small wood shavings, a pile of dead leaves or pine needles, they would smolder and eventually flare up. So far, the vigilant town folks and volunteer firefighters of Monte Vista had avoided a major disaster.

"This fire thing is out of control," Josh said to his friends one day at lunch. "It's destroying all our trees and driving the wildlife away."

"I wouldn't want to fight forest fires," his friend Jeff said. "It's dangerous work. Those firemen surrounded by fire up on Monty's Ridge? They barely escaped. If they didn't have the training and protective clothes, they would have been gone in a minute."

Karilyn was sitting at the next table, listening to the boys. "We gotta do something about this fire!"

"But what?" asked her friend Delaney, who had just moved to town from Texas. You heard those guys. It's dangerous, and you need training and gear and...."

"Uh oh!" said Jane, the third girl at the table staring at Karilynn. "I can see the wheels turning in her head," she said. "She's about to come up with one of her crazy ideas!"

Delaney agreed with Karilyn. "Enough is enough," Delaney sighed. "If we can do something, I'll sign up, no matter what the danger. That fire has already eaten up the forest around my Grandpa's house. All my favorite spots growing up are disappearing."

Karilynn sighed, "Our beautiful forest, ugh! Black and charred trees for about ump-teen thousand years. It takes a long time for a forest to grow back. We'll be old, I mean at least 30 before the forest is tall and green again."

Dark curls of hair fell across Delaney's face. She pushed them behind her ears, and groaned, "that's an awful thought!"

Karilynn's frown burst into a big smile. "I've got it! Let's do some research, get some ideas and then we can put our heads together and come up with a plan. We'll call it…Adventure Fire Out!"

***

The fire had not changed the business at the ranch since it was on the other side of Lincoln Ridge. Aunt Netta continued to take calls for information and reservations. She assured each prospective client that they were safe from the fire and business was as usual. She was a great saleswoman.

"The Hi-Lonesome Ranch is a horse training facility," Aunt Netta would explain to enquirers on the phone. "You can come with your horse and we will train you both, or just drop him off and pick him up in a few weeks trained and ready to ride. Taking part in the training is the most fun. You get a bed, great ranch cooking, and training on how to continue schooling the critter yourself."

So the ranch had stayed busy all summer and into the fall. Customers found a warm bed in a historic lodge with great mountain views. And all discovered that Aunt Natta's delicious food was well worth the price.

Work days were hectic for Grandpa, Charlie, and the other employees of the ranch. As often as possible, Mindy would sit on the fence and watch the training classes, taking notes in her mind, for when the time came that she would have her own horse to train.

Aunt Netta had her own crew to help with the lodging and the cooking. Mindy was glad that no one assumed that because she was a girl, she should be in the kitchen instead of out in the corral working with the horses. Aunt Netta encouraged her by saying, "When I was your age, I rode every time I had a free minute. Your grandpa mentioned the other day that you should be in working with me, but I reminded him of our younger sister who loved indoor chores, while I thrived helping him and our father with outdoor chores."

"What did he say to that, Aunt Netta?" Mindy asked.

She gave Mindy a big smile. "He made one of his hrumpping noises and left the kitchen. He knows better than to argue with me."

"Thanks," Mindy sighed. "I don't know what I'd do cooped up inside cooking all day. Uh…well…I mean," Mindy stopped suddenly embarrassed.

"I know what you mean, Sweetheart. No hard feelings here!"

***

Mindy's favorite day of the week was Saturday as Charlie let her assist with the Saturday Riding School. Shannon, who also loved to ride, joined her today to help with the school. As soon as Mom drove through the gate their car doors flew open even before the car rolled to a stop.

"Thanks, Mom," Mindy shouted over her shoulder as she and Shannon raced to the barn. Mindy pulled up short, surprised to see two familiar faces in the class of five kids.

With fists clinched, her anger showed on her face. Standing next to two horses, stood her least favorite people, Herm and John (or Herm and Germ as the Cunningham kids fondly called them).

"What are you doing here?" Mindy's eyes flashed with anger.

"We're buying two horses. Our Moms said we have to take riding lessons, which is dumb because I already know how to ride," Herm said.

"Me too," John…aka Germ…huffed.

Charlie was just completing his instructions to the class on how to groom their mounts before putting on blankets and saddles.

"Hi Mindy, howdy Shannon," his face crinkled up with a smile. "You two are just in time to help these little gals saddle up for the first time. Meanwhile, I'll give the boys some tips they may not know."

Mindy smiled at the two small girls who shyly told her their names. "I'm Mindy," she said, "and last year I was learning the things that you are learning today. It's easy once you get the knack! However, my friend Shannon here, she's the expert. She's ridden all of her life."

Shannon smiled at the girls. "Do you like horses?" she asked. The little ones bobbed their heads enthusiastically. "Well, that's what'll make you experts soon enough."

First, they showed them how to lay the blankets on the horse's back. Shannon was about to lift up the first saddle when she caught Charlie out of the corner of her eye….

Charlie had started with the smaller of the three boys, saying to Germ and Herm, "Follow my lead here boys. Just do what I do."

"Noth'n to this," Herm announced, and before Charlie knew what had happened, the two older boys had climbed up into their saddles.

"Hold on now, I need to check those cinches," Charlie started to say, but both boys dug their heels into their mounts' sides. Surprised by the rough treatment, the horses danced around in a cloud of dust, and then bolted off running.

Germ's cowboy hat went flying off. He had found the saddle horn and was holding on for dear life! He had not tightened his cinch correctly and found himself slipping sideways, as the loose saddle inched down the horse's side. The horse made a quick stop at the pond, and that jarred the loose saddle all the way under the horse's belly with John falling hard to the ground.

Meanwhile Herm was having his own problems. He gripped the reigns in each hand, arms extended outward like flapping bird wings.

"Whoa, whoa," he yelled, kicking his feet and yanking the reigns at the same time. The horse, of course, didn't understood these signals, he just wanted to get rid of the rider. He stopped on a dime and Herm flew over the horse's head, into the pond, with a loud splash.

"Dadburned, know-it-all kids," Charlie fumed. "Go see if they're hurt," he ordered Mindy. Rushing over to the pond, Mindy arrived in time to see the shocked and frightened faces of the two bullies. Seeing her, they both stood up quickly, put on an air of bravado while stretching their arms and legs.

"You two experts aren't hurt, are you?" Mindy laughed at the Germsters. She hollered back to Charlie that the boys were ok.

He left Shannon with the other children with instructions to "Just stay put!" and hobbled over to the boys. "Why in tarnation didn't you boys do as you were told?" Charlie growled at the two. He snatched up each boy, and poked and punched their arms, legs, and body in search of serious injuries.

When he found none, he directed the boys to lead the horses back to the barn.

"Wasn't our fault," Germ muttered sharply yanking the bridle.

"Yea, these dumb horses don't follow directions," Herm chimed in. He kicked his horse as hard as he could.

Mindy squeezed her eyes shut not believing what she saw. She opened them and saw the storm gathering on Charlie's face.

Clinching his fists at his side, Charlie fought the rage he was feeling inside.

Teeth clinched, and his eyes alight with fireworks, he grabbed the reigns from the two boys and put them in Mindy's hands. "Bring them along, Mindy. These two brats and I have some issues to work out."

At the barn, Charlie turned the class over to Mindy and Shannon. "Show them how to unsaddle the horses. Then have each one saddle up again and walk their horses over to the ring. We'll work on riding skills in there today. I'll be back soon."

Turning to the younger kids, Charlie said, "I trust you students will do as you are told!" Seeing his fierce expression, three heads nodded obediently at Charlie's words.

With a firm grip on each boy's arm, Charlie dragged the sulking kids toward the house.

"Phew! I'm glad I'm not in their shoes," Mindy said to Shannon.

***

That evening Aunt Netta, with Karilynn's assistance, had set the table in the large dining room for a special dinner for all of the employees at the ranch. The past two weeks had seen a full house. But now they had arranged to have a few days off to catch their breath. Josh and Karilynn joined Mindy and Shannon who were invited to stay for the big meal.

Soon, every room would be occupied with new clients and the barn full of fresh horses to train. The new clients were mostly city folks eager to learn how to train their own horses so they could get in touch with their "western side."

"It's always easier," Charlie sighed over dinner, "when the customers are country folks who already have a little experience with animals."

Charlie continued entertaining the group with stories of the past week. "The worst came today… two kids from town. I first met up with them at Outdoor School. I don't think I've ever met ruder kids in all my days," Charlie moaned. "They said they knew all about horses, but they didn't know one thing about saddles, bridles, or riding."

"They know everything," Josh smirked. "Just ask them."

"Just listen, Josh," Mindy poked him quietly.

As Charlie described the dust, sliding saddles and flying arms, ending with one boy on the ground and the other in the pond, Josh's eyes sparkled with glee.

"It's not funny," Grandpa's blue eyes flashed.

Grandpa's grouchy nature made Mindy mad. Angry words formed in her mind, but all she said was, "No one was hurt, Grandpa, although I thought Charlie might …"

"If they had been hurt," Grandpa interrupted, "it would have meant big trouble for me. Dad-gummed parents would have given me a lot of grief, maybe even sued the ranch."

Mindy, chastened, said no more as she sat fuming in her chair staring at the hot plate of food.

"So much alike, those two," mused Charlie watching Grandpa and Mindy's exchange. "Well," he said out loud. "It wasn't funny at the time, Mr. Cunningham, but I can see why the kids loved seeing those two get their comeuppance! They're mean ones all right, and troublemakers. I don't think their parents will have much to say. I set them straight."

"And when Charlie sets you straight, you stay straight!" Josh said quietly with a grin.

CHAPTER 7

TEDDY BEAR DAY

Mindy and Josh waited at the bus stop with the early-morning blaaas. Weighed down by a backpack full of undone homework, Josh shook his head and grimaced at Karilyn's bright-eyed cheerfulness.

"Today is *Teddy Bear Day* for the third grade," she smiled. "And you have to act like a regular stuffed bear...no talking!" Karilynn looked into the eyes of her brown bear and then gave BF Bear a big hug.

"Whoah, I know that." the bear growled. Karilynn gave him another hug and twirled him around by his ear.

"Here we go," said Mindy, as the school bus came lumbering down the hill. "This should be an interesting ride with our two self-proclaimed expert cowboys on board," she smirked.

"How are you gonna' handle this? I'd let it go if I were you," Josh instructed Mindy. "The further away we stay from those two, the better off we'll be!"

"I'm not saying a word!" The bus rolled to a stop and the doors swished open. The three children stepped onto the bus and sat several rows behind Herm and Germ.

"Phew! What's that smell, John?"

"Whoo-ee! I don't know." Both boys sniffed. "I think it's manure. In my opinion, somebody needs to change her perfume." John turned up his nose up and sniffed again.

Mindy bit her lip, but said nothing.

"Nah, I think someone's been spending way too much time with horses. Hey, Mr. Bus Driver! Isn't there a rule about horsey smelling students on the school bus?"

Benjamin Franklin Bear gave a low growl, and Josh jumped to his feet. Mindy pulled him back down. She could fight her own battles. "I tried to be quiet, I really did," Mindy muttered under her breath as she jumped up.

"Better than smelling like a chicken coop. I see two wanna-be cowboys who are really just chickenboys," Mindy shot back and then gave a chicken squawk… "bruuuk, buck, buck."

The tension on the bus shot up a few notches, but the two boys seemed to back off.

A few minutes later Herm leaned over to Germ and whispered loudly for the kids to hear. "Dumb people must run in that family. Look at that sissy girl bringing her teddy bear to school."

A flash of brown moved down the aisle quickly, grabbed two ears, smacked two heads together, and returned to his seat so fast that Mindy, Josh, and Karilynn hardly realized what happened.

"Ouch!" howled Herm.

"Hey!" wailed the Germ! "That hurt!" Both boys, rubbing their heads, turned around with fireworks in their eyes.

Cluck, cluck," squawked the brown bear, who sat perched on Karilynn's lap. He emphasized his point with a ferocious growl.

Germ and Herm gaped open-mouth at BF Bear, and then quickly turned around, not believing what they had just heard or seen. When Germ sneaked a peek over his shoulder all he saw was a floppy stuffed bear with a smirk on his face.

The bus stopped and eight more school kids climbed on board. The five feuding children completed the trip in silence. When the bus finally arrived at school, Herm and Germ remained glued to their seats. Josh and Karilynn got off the bus, but Mindy stopped by the two boys' seats. "Now I'm not telling any chickenboy tales around school. I'm not like that. But you had better stay away from me and my family!"

***

After school, Karilynn asked her teacher, Mrs. Hines, if she could do a special report on the forest fire for extra credit.

"What kind of report are you thinking about?" Mrs. Hines asked curiously.

"Well, fire fighting," Karilynn said, looking thoughtful. "Mostly on the firemen who are working here trying to protect us. I think all Monte Vista families should know about our local heroes. Like where they come from, are they ever afraid when fighting big fires, what tools they use…bits and pieces of stuff like that. I could make it interesting, I know I could!" Karilyn exclaimed!

Karilynn's main plan was to find out all she could about forest fires and figure out a way for her friends to help the firemen put an end to the Lincoln Ridge fire. "I won't mention that until I figure out everything we need to know," Karilynn thought to herself.

"I know you'd do a fine paper," the smiling teacher said. "You can do that during our extra credit projects the class will be writing soon." She knew how much Karilynn loved to explore new ideas. Even at her young age, Mrs Hines found she did very good research!

That night, everyone was discussing Karilynn's new project at the dinner table.

"I think you should find out about arson dogs. Lots of regions have dogs trained to seek out where a fire started and what material was used," Mindy said.

"I'm not sure they have dogs trained to deal with forest fires," Mom said thoughtfully, "but it's certainly an interesting idea to research."

"If I had to listen to your report, I'd wanna' know about some of the special equipment they use," Josh interjected. "Especially about the choppers and those cool C130 planes that they use to fight the fires from the air."

"Lets see, firedogs, special equipment, airplanes and helicopters for fire fighting from the air," wrote Karilynn. "Helmets, firefighter's uniforms, fire trucks," she wrote finishing her list.

The next day when Karilynn was reading her list to her friends before school, Shannon and Mindy were listening nearby. "Why don't you go and interview one of the firefighters?" Shannon asked. "Couldn't your friend Doc Stephens talk Mr. Smoklin into setting up an interview?"

"Interview?" asked Karilyn looking puzzled

"You know," Mindy added. "Like what a reporter does on TV. Talk to one of the firefighters in person. Ask him questions and write down what he says for your report. That's a great idea, Shannon."

"Oohhh," said Karilynn excitedly. "Do you think that Doc would talk Mr. Smoklin into getting me an interview?"

"Well, you won't know unless you ask," Mindy answered.

After school, Karilynn and Mindy rushed over to Doc's cabin. Josh had football practice that kept him from going with the girls. But oh, how he wanted to go! Meeting a fireman would be awesome!

"I'm sure Smoky and I can fixed that up," Doc answered, when the girls excitedly presented him their proposal.

Amazingly, with just one phone call, Doc had the interview set up for the very next Saturday with a fireman named Tuck.

"We'll do it after your football game, so you can go with us Josh," Karilynn assured her brother.

Josh looked at Karilynn with a big smile. "Hey thanks!" Josh exclaimed. "I'll have to remember to be nicer to my sister," he thought to himself.

***

It seemed like the school week crawled by…but Saturday finally arrived.

That morning the whole family was at Josh's football game. Josh came out of the locker room wearing a big smile after the game. "Two touchdowns, and Tugboat even slapped me on the back."

"Mitaah fine game, Cunninhaam," Josh mimicked the coach's Texas accent. "That's as good as it gets, coming from Coach," Josh was beaming with pleasure.

"Hop in," Doc hollered to the kids and waved good-bye to Mrs. Cunningham. On the forty-five minute drive to the Fire Command Center at Taylor Reservoir, the crew chatted happily about the game and Josh's touchdowns.

Except for Karilynn. She was going over the questions in her head she would ask the fireman. She patted the backpack on her lap as if to assure herself that everything she needed was in there. Notes, pencils, pens, and most importantly a list of questions she planned to ask. Inside her backpack were all the important tools she needed for the investigation she was doing for Adventure Fire-Out.

"Are you going to eat that chicken leg?" Josh nudged Karilyn, pointing at her last piece. Mom had been busy in the kitchen the night before cooking up food. Lots of food. This was a sure sign that she was worrying about the trip her kids were taking so close to the fire.

Although Josh had eaten several pieces of fried chicken, potato salad, and coleslaw, he was hungrily eyeing Karilynn's chicken. "You can have it, Josh. I'm too excited to eat," replied Karilyn.

Mindy and Shannon were munching out on brownies and sugar cookies they had found packed in the picnic basket. When Fireman Tuck has a bite of your Mom's famous brownies, he'll be glad to give you an interview," Shannon laughed. "At least as long as the cookies hold out!"

"No way is he going to be able to eat all of those cookies," Doc said. "Your mom made enough to feed a whole fire brigade."

"Look!" Josh pointed to the sky just over Tin Cup Pass. It was dark, dark gray, and even though it was miles away, you could smell the burning trees. The loud, whirling noise of a helicopter sounded in their ears. As their eyes surveyed the skies, they saw the chopper moving into the smoke.

Seeing where the actual fire was burning felt a little scary. Josh felt chills creep up his spine. "You know, if you hiked 30 miles further north on the Colorado Trail from our cabin, your would come down into that campground and lake on Cottonwood Pass. That's too close for comfort."

Driving around one more bend in the road revealed a huge camp. There were hundreds of white pup tents, all neatly set up in rows. At the center of this large campsite was a huge doublewide trailer. The kids captured a whiff of the delicious smells of food cooking, competing with the caustic smells blowing in from the fire area.

At each end of the camp were a line of Port-a-Potties and additional trailers with showers inside. To the west, a little ways from the campsite and woods, sat a huge helicopter.

Karilynn slung her backpack over her shoulder as they walked over to a makeshift meeting room in a large green tent. A tall man in blue jeans and a plaid flannel shirt headed their way. His face was covered with dark soot.

"Hey guys, you must be Doc Stephens?" He reached out to shake Doc's hand. "And this must be your group who came to interview me about fighting forest fires." He shook the small hand that Karilynn had stuck out in his direction.

"I'm the head researcher," announced Karilynn respectfully. "Are you Mr. Tuck? Mr. Smoklin told me to ask for Fireman Tuck."

"That's me," he said with a tired smile. "As you can see, I just came in off the line. Had a small emergency that delayed me from washing up before our meeting time. Do you have time to wait while I clean up a bit?"

"You bet," said Doc. "No hurry on our side. We can grab a coke and look around."

"Hey, here comes a guy you would like to meet," Mr. Tuck said, as he eyed a man who had just come into the tent. "Hey, Big Jake. Come on over here and meet these folks."

"He's our helicopter pilot," Mr. Tuck pointed out. "I bet you could talk him into showing you his chopper and how it's specially equipped to fight fires."

"Wow!" was all that Josh could say.

The man looked at his watch. "I don't go back on duty for thirty minutes. That should give us enough time," Big Jake said, as he introduced himself.

"As for me, the right amount of time to clean up. See you kids back here in thirty minutes." Mr. Tuck gave Josh a big wink and strode off towards a row of tents.

***

Big Jake grabbed Karilynn's hand, and motioned for the rest of the group to follow him out to his chopper. "Oh, this is much bigger than it looks from the highway," Karilynn said in awe.

"Mr., uh, Mr. Big Jake...." Josh began. He was dying to ask the pilot all about the helicopter.

"Just call me Jake," the fireman said with a smile! "This is a Bell 205," he said as he walked the group around the helo, showing them the tanks that had been added to release fire retardant. Josh asked a million questions and Jake patiently answered all of them. With wide eyes, the children excitedly climb on board the craft when Big Jake invited them on board. There were tons of gauges, and other cool stuff that Jake pointed out to the kids. Then, to top it all off, he demonstrated how to fly a helicopter.

Thirty minutes raced by. Jake started up the helicopter with the whoop, whoop of the blades as the engine started to rev up.

The sound of motors put a dent in their talking. Jake's eyes caught sight of Mr. Tuck down below and he held up four fingers, and then pointed down to alert Doc and Mr. Tuck that the kids would be climbing down.

Turning in his seat, Jake gave the kids a salute and gave Karilynn a big thumbs up as she moved toward the steps. Josh lingered behind, hoping for an invitation to fly with Jake. Big Jake gave him a knowing smile, but pointed sharply towards the door. Josh smiled, saluted and climbed down the steps as he mouthed, "Thank you, Jake."

Fireman Tuck pulled Josh into the circle of folks that were standing close to him. He shouted at Josh above the roar of the engine, "Stay close to me. Let's go!" Tuck herded the group away from the helicopter, and gave Jake the high sign that they were safely away. The helicopter slowly lifted into the sky and then flew off toward the smoking fire.

CHAPTER 8

FIREFIGHTERS LIFELINE

Fireman Tuck led the group back into the big dining tent. "I'm going to get a drink," he said, "and then we'll sit down and talk. Who wants an cherry limeade? It's the house specialty here." Inquisitive faces turned his way as he walked across the room. "Oh come on guys, you know...when you mix limeade with a squirt of cherry phosphate" All agreed that a cherry limeade sounded good, and he soon returned with the drinks.

Karilynn had set out her notebook and pen along with her list of questions. She took out a flower-covered paper plate and arranged brownies and cookies neatly on it.

"You're going to be glad you let this little girl interview you when you taste her Mom's world famous brownies," Doc exclaimed, reaching for one himself.

"I'll take payment in chocolate for an interview any old day," Fireman Tuck said with a big smile. "Start shooting your questions little lady, cause I can eat brownies and talk at the same time."

"Lets see...Name," Karilynn wrote on her page, "Mr. Tuck... and where do you call home when you're not fighting fires?"

"Call me Sam, darling, and I will call you Karilynn. Not married, no kids," he continued while peeking at her page of notes. "I'm from right around here…Bailey, Colorado, to be exact. Although most of my firefighting buddies come from all over the United States."

Karilynn nodded in reply. "First of all, I would like to find out what type of special equipment is required to fight a fire this big."

"This girl really wants to know about fires," the firefighter thought to himself as he took in her somber tone and serious eyes.

He adjusted his attitude to match hers, because firefighting is a serious business…his business. And the more boys and girls understood fires, the safer our forest will be that future generations would be inheriting.

"Each piece of our equipment is very important and designed to protect us from the fierce heat and smoke of a forest fire." He reached under the table and pulled out some equipment he had stashed there to show the kids.

"Our boots are made from waterproof, flame-resistant leather," Fireman Tuck said as he plunked down a huge boot for his rather large feet on the table. "These HexArmor gloves are thermal-lined and made from the same kind of leather as our boots."

As Sam was talking, he turned and showed them his backpack. "We all carry some sort of SCBA breathing apparatus depending on the intensity and size of the fire. Finally we have our fire retardant pants and hood," he said while displaying the items on the table. "That's about it, I think," Sam said, as took two more cookies from the plate.

Karilynn looked puzzled and Sam followed her eyes that were glued to his head. "Oh yeah, I forgot my head gear. This is our specially designed fire and rescue helmet with full communications," he said fishing under the table. He pulled it out and plopped it onto his head.

"What would be important for us to know about your job, Mr. Tuck?" Karilynn questioned in her no-nonsense voice.

"Well..." he said slowly, thinking about his answer, and taking another brownie. "Fighting forest fires is extremely dangerous. You don't want to get surrounded by fire, or be unable to make your way back to the fire perimeter. Oh, and that reminds me of another piece of equipment we always have with us a fire tent. If, somehow, we do need to take cover against a fast moving fire, we have our safety shelter with us. We just hope that we will never have to use it. It's sort of a last resort piece of equipment that means you're in real trouble."

"We have to be aware at all times where the fire is burning and how fast it's burning. A forest fire burns faster on the outer edges, and sometimes it just hops from treetop to treetop. That's called a crown fire, which is a rapid moving fire. Another type of fire is one fed by flash fuels. That is what we call grass, leaves, pine needles, and old dead trees on the ground. It gobbles those elements up like I do brownies," the fireman smiled "That's the hottest fire, and it moves faster than a NASCAR driver."

As he took another brownie, he glanced at the faces of the children. Each one was listening, totally absorbed in his explanation.

"Hey! I'm the only one eating cookies. Someone better help me out here," Sam said.

The kids grabbed another cookie, except for Karilynn, who was busily writing in her notebook.

"What about wind, Sam?" Mindy asked. "I've heard it has a lot to do with the direction and speed of a fire."

"And tell us about your helicopters, too," Josh mumbled through a mouth full of brownie.

"Wind is our greatest enemy," Sam said. "It can blow a fire faster than we can fight it. Wind can cause the flames to jump over a road or stream and start the fire in a new place. Often times, when a fireman gets trapped behind lines, it's because the wind has made the movement of the fire unpredictable."

"On the other hand, Josh," the helicopter is one of our greatest friends. Helitack crews are trained to fight from the air, just as Joe explained to you. Spewing fire-retardant material on the trees battles flames in a way that can't be duplicated from the ground."

"Are you on the Helitack crew?" Shannon asked.

"No, that's Jake's job. I'm the team leader on a Hot Shot Crew. We get sent into the heart of the fire. Our job is to scrape out firebreaks so the flames will not be able to jump from one place to another. We also set up provisional control lines which is an area where other firemen can fight the fires. Instead of a helicopter, we use axes and shovels to get our job done."

Mr. Tuck stopped to catch his breath. "Two of the happiest words in a firefighter's vocabulary are *"fire contained."* That means the fire is not moving or growing bigger. Then we can focus on putting the fire out in the contained area. After that, we can close up camp and head for home. Enough information for you, Karilynn?"

"Well, one more question," she answered. "How does it feel to fight a forest fire. Are you ever scared?"

"I'm scared all the time, every fire. Being scared is what keeps us alert and keeps us alive."

"I bet it takes a lot of courage to fight forest fires," Mindy said.

"A cowboy friend of mine says "courage is not running away when things look bad," replied Fireman Tuck.

"What can we do to help you, I mean…your team, well, any of the firefighters," Karilynn stuttered out. Her mind was spinning, as her real reason for meeting this man was to get her and her friends on the fire fighting team.

"My friends and I want to help in putting this fire out," Karilynn rushed on. "We can shovel fire breaks or maybe walk the forest looking for hot spots.

"Or we could ride in the helicopters as an extra pair of eyes to help the pilot with his job," Josh exclaimed excitedly.

Sam and Doc looked at each other in surprise! "You mean work close to the flames?" the fireman asked.

"Be in the line of fire?" Doc added nervously.

"That's a good one, Doc," Josh laughed.

"I didn't mean it as a joke, Josh." Doc shot back in a sharp tone. "You can't be in the area of the fire. It's dangerous, fire is very dangerous! You kids know that!"

Sam held up his hand. "Now just a minute, Doc!" Turning to the kids he said, "I understand that you guys want to help."

"Yes," Shannon interrupted. "That fire is getting way too close to my Grandpa's house and to a lot of our friends' houses, too."

"We know if we asked our friends to help on Project Fire-Out, (that's what we would call it) we would get lots of volunteers," Karilynn said, fearlessly eyeing Doc. She looked pleadingly into fireman Tuck's face.

"Wow," Sam said sitting back in his seat. You're a bunch of gutsy kids. With a great and brave idea," he said solemnly, nodding his head in thought.

"Great idea, but impossible," Doc barked.

Sam held up both hands for Doc to be quiet. He sat looking at the children, pondering their plucky offer.

"I'm sorry, you guys," he said after a few minutes. "There are things that Project Fire-Out could do. But it would not involve actual fire fighting. I'm sure if you think about it, you would understand that we can't put civilians in that kind of danger."

Sam saw all the disappointed faces as he looked around the group.

"But you said there were some things we could do, Sam," Josh pointed out.

"Yeah…. I was so surprised that a bunch of kids would like to help out, that I had to think about it. But three things popped into my mind right away. All firefighters have these two problems in common. They're always hungry, and they are lonely for their family back home."

"Well, maybe we could get Moms and kids to help in the kitchen," Karilynn said thoughtfully.

"Nah, Karilynn. Professional crews cook for them," Josh replied knowingly. "What do you mean?" he questioned Sam.

"Snack cooks! These brownies gave me the idea…"Project-Fire Out" would lift a firemen's spirits with homemade snacks. I mean real snacks! Not processed stuff like what's in those vending machines. As you can see, we have plenty of that stuff around here." He waved his hand in the direction of the dispenser machines. "But I haven't tasted anything like these brownies for ages. If you want your firemen to know that you love 'em, homemade snacks are where it's at!"

Sam looked over and spotted Karilynn busily writing notes in her notebook. He smiled, feeling proud of his ideas, while reaching for the last brownie.

"What about homesickness?" Mindy asked. "You said the firefighters are often homesick, and I'm not sure how we can help out with that."

"Well, began Fireman Tuck, thinking as he talked. With a few more computers, we could add Skype stations here in the dining room instead of all the guys having to line up in the communications tent."

"How would we ever raise the money for more computers?" Josh asked, thinking of his meager allowance.

"Josh! We'll earn the money…by fundraisers…car washes, bake sales, an all-school garage sale!" Karilynn's mind raced ahead of her pencil and all the smiling faces showed they were in agreement.

"And one more thing," Sam said, mulling it over, "We need crews of volunteers to seek out wounded and displaced animals. At a safe distance, of course," he murmured in Doc's direction. "They could then radio the Forest Service and keep watch until these animals were moved to safety. It would be a great help to find these animals for us. If they don't need to be moved, they need to be fed daily, until they find new sources of food after the fires are put out."

"So, that's it," the big fireman concluded. 'Snack cooks, computers with Skype, and animal rescue!" Sam looked longingly at the empty plate.

"That ought to keeps you kids busy!" Doc said with a smile. He mouthed a "thank you" to Fireman Tuck.

"We need to go and let you rest, Mr. Tuck," Karilyn instructed the group in her most grown-up voice. She stuck out her small hand to shake his big one. "We'll get Project Fire-Out started right away." After "thank yous" and handshakes were shared all around, Mr. Tuck helped load the kids in the van. Doc started the engine and turned the van towards home. Karilynn looked back and saw Mr. Tuck waving goodbye, and she waved back in return. "We will be back soon," she silently promised the fireman and herself.

***

Doc smiled as he looked into the back of the van full of sleeping kids. He had no clue of the danger that would soon surround the Cunningham family.

Dinner was ready when they got back home and Doc was easily talked into sticking around for some of Mrs Cunningham's world famous chicken fried steak and smashed taters.

Mrs. Cunningham was naturally curious and concerned about her kids trip to the fire front. They never would have managed to go if Doc wouldn't have offered to drive. Doc innocently asked Sherry if she had heard about Karilyn's Project Fire-Out.

All three kids responded with a variety of diversions…Karilyn loudly asked where the banana cream pie was while Josh coughed into his hand and tapped Doc under the table. Mindy mumbled about Project Fire-Out being a book report they were planning as all three grabbed dishes and headed to the kitchen. No telling what mom would cook if she found out about Project Fire-Out.

CHAPTER 9

THE ENEMY ATTACKS

Well it didn't take long before the kids found out what Mom thought of Project Fire-Out. But, after numerous days of cajoling and pleading, Mom and Doc finally relented and Project Fire-Out was off and running with their reluctant blessing.

Which eventually led to Karilynn looking at a kitchen-full of kids at the Cottonwood Lake Base camp "What is your team doing here, Timo?"

Timothy looked up at Karilynn. "I looked at the schedule," he said, "and today is our day to help out in the kitchen."

"Well, I wrote the schedule and this is our day to work in the kitchen. I have a friend who says 'Too many kids with their fingers in the cookie dough makes a big mess and no cookies.'" Karilynn eyed the kitchen full of laughing and shoving kids.

"No, no, this will never do," she muttered to herself. Suddenly, one of her "bright ideas" popped into her mind. "Has your Dad left yet?" she asked Timo.

"Yeah, he drove up, we hopped out and off he went," Timo replied.

"Hmm," she said thinking. "We'll head on out and Team Timo can stay here! Hey," she shouted, trying to be heard over the clamor of the crowded kitchen.

Timo put two fingers in his mouth and gave a shrill whistle that got everyone's attention. "I have changed today's plans," Karilynn shouted. "Timo's team will stay here and help in the kitchen and my team will meet outside at the water tanks now. We've got other work to do." Karilynn's team began to file out of the kitchen and into the parking lot.

"What other work?" Josh asked skeptically. He wanted to be with his friends that were left to work in the kitchen.

"I don't know yet," she replied. "We'll figure something out. But that just wasn't gonna work! Too many kids with their fingers' in the cookie…"

"I know, I know," Josh sighed. "Messes and nothing gets done."

"Well, what are we going to do?" asked Mindy and Shannon who had been listening in on their conversation.

"Well, I'm not sure," she said with a worried frown. "I don't want to let our volunteers down." Just then Karilynn's face lit up as she spotted fireman Tuck heading their way.

She and Josh raced up to see him, and explained their dilemma. "I don't want the kids to get frustrated and drop out of the Fire-Out program," Karilynn moaned as she explained what had happen. "You know kids," she said with a grim look.

Fireman Tuck held up his hand. "Yes, I see your problem, but there's always work to do. I have a job that I believe your team is ready for. You can go join the high school guys that are working on the fire break. They'll be glad to have your help."

The kids all popped into the back of Mr. Tuck's pickup as he roared out of the camp heading towards the fire break. The kids buzzed with excitement because it would be the first time the younger kids could work on the fire break. They could see the smoke off to the west, but the truck headed southeast toward town.

They pulled up at a place 20 miles outside of Monte Vista. There were the dusty trucks and cars of the high school students who had liked Karilynn's idea and started an older Fire-Out team. As Mr. Tuck parked along the road, they could hear voices close by.

The fireman gave boxes to several kids to carry. As they followed the voices, Karilynn's team found the boys resting in the shaded woods. Mr. Tuck pulled out sodas and doughnuts and while the high school team dug into the snack, he explained the new plan for the day.

Some of the older boys looked doubtful as he assigned each one with a buddy-helper from Karilynn's group. "You have to take orders from your buddy," he explained to the younger kids. "Do whatever he says so you can be of assistance and not a hindrance to this hard working team. They're one of my best."

After Tuck left, the head of the group, Ketch, began to bark out orders. Ketch's real name was John, but his nickname came from his ketchup-red hair. He passed out shovels and rakes and instructed the big buddies to show each newby how to prepare the ground for the fire break.

"We're building this big fire break all along here as a precaution against the fire making it into town. We hope that it won't come this way, but if it does, this will help the firefighters control it at this point."

As the buddies moved off to their work site, the leader looked down at Karilynn. "And what am I suppose to do with you, Shrimp?" he asked, smiling down at Karilynn.

She frowned at the tall boy and held out her hand for his rake. "We'll see who's still moving dirt when it's time to quit, Ketch."

At the end of the day, both teams were surprised at how much work they had accomplished. While exhausted, the compliments that the big buddies paid to Karilynn's team boosted their spirits. "I've only got this Little Shrimp for my buddy," said Ketch, "but, I'm betting she is the best firefighter in the whole town." For the first time that day, Karilynn's face lit up in a big smile.

At school, The Big and The Little Buddies started hanging out together. They ate lunch together, worked on fundraising projects together, and even school work. Other teams copied the group efforts that the first Buddy Team had developed. Some of the new Buddy Teams worked with Mr. Smoklin on feeding displaced animals the forest service was rounding up.

Principal Noble, patting his stomach with pride, walked daily through the hallways bragging to anyone who would listen about the cooperative work bringing the older and younger students together.

The very Saturday that Karilynn and Ketch's teams were to return to work on the fire break closest to town, a picture of the "Flame Outs" and a smiling Principal Noble (hand proudly on stomach) appeared in the local paper. Karilynn, as the organizer of the Fire-Out project, explained how the Fire Buddy System was developed through the Fire-Out program.

Fireman Tuck rewarded the arrival of the hard working team with high fives and special treats. Sodas and Pizzas were loaded in the trucks for their morning break.

As he did everyday, Tuck pulled the two units aside and went over Safety Rules. By now, the kids knew the rules by heart. But Tuck had them repeat each one and explain why they were important. He helped them load up their equipment and waved them on their way, convinced they would be safe and diligent helpers.

***

Josh and Mindy and their buddies parked at the orange flag markers where the fire break work had ended yesterday. The wind had picked up and Mindy pulled her hair back into a pony tail as she started to work.

Karilynn and Ketch's team parked a half mile closer to town and piled out of the truck, anxious to start work. Mindy and Josh's team and Ketch and Karilynn's team worked towards each other, competing to see which one could cover more ground. This race kept them working at full speed. This secret strategy kept the firemen wondering how the kids got so much work done in such a short time. The wind continued to build and they brought out their bandanas to cover every thing but their eyes.

"We're beating them now!" Ketch shouted. "Put your back into it guys...that wind won't slow us down."

Karilynn stopped to push her hair behind her ears and out of her eyes. Just then, she felt a big shove from behind. "Hey," she fussed and quickly turned around, looking for the culprit.

She saw a huge moose and a stuffed bear hanging on to his horn. "What's that for," she asked as the moose nodded his head up and down and stomped his huge hoofs. The stomping caused

the bear to hang on for dear life. "Look over theerrrrrrreee......."
the bear shouted. But the wind swept the bear's voice away.

"Don't move," he shouted into the moose's ear. He punctuated
the command with a couple of paw slaps to the moose's head.

The small bear slid courageously down the moose's long nose with
only his bottom paw hooked around the horn. "Look out behind you,"
he growled in his loudest voice. Karilynn had walked up close to the
animals and saw the bear pointing his paw behind her to the forest.

"Fire," she screamed running to her team. Ketch and the other
team members looked where she was pointing. Burning embers
filled the air. When they looked down toward Josh and Mindy's
position, they could see actual flames creeping up the road.

"You go for help while I warn the other kids," Ketch ordered
his team. "Go with our team, Shrimp. I'll bring the others in their
truck." Not looking back, Ketch switched into full gear, racing
towards the other group. When he got close to their worksite, his
heart fell. His friends were nowhere to be seen. Had they been
caught in the woods while resting or finishing their snack?

"Hey, Ketch," he heard a shout. Realizing it came from behind
the truck, he rushed over relieved to find that they were at least
aware of the danger.

Karilynn had looked back to make sure that her two animals
friends were moving towards safety. Then she ran as fast as she
could after Ketch. She was the fastest girl in her class, but still no
match for her friend's long legs.

"That dadgum truck won't start," Josh moaned, as the teenager
in charge tried to start it again. As the motor turned over with a
whine, Ketch could tell that they were going nowhere in that truck!

"Get out, grab the fire tents and go across the road," Ketch
commanded. His whole body was shaking, but as the oldest he
knew he had to take charge.

"Don't we need to move further on down the road away from the truck and its gas tank?" Mindy questioned.

"Good idea," Ketch exclaimed. "Move it guys, get further down the road! We'll use our firebreak, the natural dip in the road, and our tents for protection."

"But," Josh said in a voice that shook with fear.

"No buts, Josh…Just do it!"

"But," Josh exclaimed again, as he pointed and started running down the road away from his team.

"Shrimp!" Ketch shouted as he looked where Josh was pointing. In three long steps Ketch grabbed Josh by the collar. "I'm faster, I'll get her. You're in charge of making sure the fire tents are properly set up."

In a matter of seconds he reached Karilynn, snatched her up and raced toward the group. "Get under," Josh was yelling and pushing the group under a large tent. Mindy balked at going under the shelter without her sister. "We've got her," Josh reported, as he saw his small sister in Ketch's big arms. "We'll get under the other tent." Mindy eyed the growing flames and crawled under her tent.

"You've got them set-up right," Ketch said, sounding relieved. They ducked under the small second tent, and lay down on the ground. They pushed Karilynn between them as if their bodies could provide extra protection. "Shrimp! I told you to go…Why didn't you go?" Ketch groaned. They could hear the tears in his voice.

"She would never leave us like that!" Joshed exclaimed. Karilynn didn't answer. She just huddled against Ketch and Josh and bravely stifled her sobs.

***

Before Ketch's team arrived in town they were amazed to see fire trucks with sirens blaring, racing towards the fire they had just left. Following the trucks was a Hummer driven by a grimed-face man with flashing eyes and wild grey eyebrows.

If his team could have seen the old man's passenger, a stuffed brown bear, it would have answered their question as to how the firemen had received the news before they made it to town.

Sheltered under the tents, all of the kids from teens down to Karilynn, huddled together, clinging to each other and hoping that their shelters would protect them. The closer the fire got to them, the hotter it got in the tents. Ketch was muttering and Karilynn realized he was praying. "Doc does that at scary times too," she thought. "Help us God," she sobbed, gripping the boys hands.

Whether fear or the wind kept them from hearing the blaring sirens, the children did not know that help had arrived until they felt the cooling water spraying over their tents. Outside, the firemen attacked the blaze that had only been held back from the tents by the fire break and the road. Inside, no one moved. Tears filled their eyes, as the relief from the heat alerted them that they were about to be rescued. Outside, grown men and firemen's black faces were streaked with tears.

When it was finally safe, Fireman Tuck, Doc, and Mr. Smoklin were the first to uncover the scared kids. One by one, they were pulled out of the tent, poked and examined. They were loaded into the Hummer and other trucks, taken to the MV hospital, where the poking and examining started all over again. Each one was assigned a bed and overnight stay with their parents to hover over them. They all wanted to leave but they still needed monitoring for the shock that was clearly seen in their eyes.

BF Bear lay clutched in Karilynn's arms while she slept. His eyes were open and alert. Two bees buzzed around Josh and Mindy guarding the two sleeping children.

In the hall, Doc stood close to Fireman Tuck, whispering comforting words to the seasoned fireman who had had the spark knocked out of him by the close encounter of his Fire-Out helpers. While the remaining firemen worked to contain the flames outside of town, the hospital finally took on an air of quiet relief.

CHAPTER 10

FAMILY SKI ADVENTURES

Mindy woke up with a start. She could feel the heat, smell the smoke, and even see the grey ash floating down outside her window. Then, she lay back on her pillow, her heart still racing. She remembered she was in her own room, the days of the fire danger long past. The grey ash was actually soft, white snowflakes, which had arrived for the Thanksgiving holidays.

Six weeks after the fire had begun, the hardworking firefighters had finally contained the fire and diligently searched for "hot spots" until the fire was declared officially out. Hundreds of acres of forest were a blackened scar on the mountain sides. It would remain scarred for years to come, but the folks of the area were grateful there were no deaths and very little structural damage.

The firemen were honored heroes. Fireman Tuck was named *Our Super Hero* of MV Schools. A huge plaque hung in the school honoring Karilynn's Fire-Out Program. Another one had been placed in the forest where the fire had started.

"Mindy, are you awake? We gotta get up and get ready for school," Karilynn yawned.

Mindy brushed the hair out of her eyes and pushed away the thoughts that had awakened her. "There's no school today, silly. Remember it's the Turkey Bird Holidays and Dad's going with us on the school ski trip!"

Fifteen minutes later they stood in the kitchen, dressed in long underwear, turtlenecks, t-shirts, heavy sweaters and jeans. "I feel like a stuffed wiener," Mindy said, struggling to settle everything into its place.

"And I'm already sweating, and I don't even have my coat on yet," Josh said, pulling his turtleneck away from his neck."

"Well, shuck off a few things," Mom instructed. "You can't ski without eating."

"Morning dear, morning kiddos!" Mr. Cunningham exclaimed, as he entered the breakfast room with a big smile on his face.

"Morning, Dad," Karilynn scooted from behind the table and threw her arms around his neck. After their close call with the fire, Mr. Cunningham had returned home for an indefinite stay with his still traumatized family.

Mr. Cunningham kissed Karilynn on her head. "Mmmm! Something smells mighty good." He gave his wife a big hug and peaked over her head to see what was cooking.

"You're still going skiing with us, right, Dad?" Josh asked.

"You bet," Dad beamed. All of the Cunningham children were thrilled to have their dad at home once again. It had been months since the family was all together under the same roof.

"Sit down guys," Mom said. "We're having pancakes, eggs, bacon, sausage, blueberry muffins, and fruit salad.

"Ohhhhh," Joshed mouthed to the girls. This huge amount of cooking meant that Mom was still upset from their close adventure with death. The woman was known to cook furiously when upset.

"And, I've already packed your ski lunches. Mindy, you and Karilynn have chicken salad sandwiches...Dad and Josh have ham and cheese. Each bag has home made potato chips, celery and carrots for your salad, and Dad, I baked your favorite dessert... Congo squares."

"Ahhh, sometimes I forget my wonderful wife and her delicious home cooked meals when I'm away in the jungles...." He was cut short by a stern look from Mom.

After breakfast and with more layers added, Karilynn hugged her Mom good-by and whispered, "Don't worry, Mom. Dad and I will bring everybody back safe!"

"Thanks for breakfast Sherry and now we're off on our Great Ski Adventure," Dad said as he slid back his chair.

Mom watched out the window as four shining faces hopped in the car and waved good-bye. "Oh my," she said worriedly. "I need to stop this worrying. I'll sit down, plan dinner and go buy groceries. Let's see....Roast beef, mashed potatoes, gravy, hot rolls, carrots, corn, blueberry and lettuce salad. Dessert: lemon pie, she listed on the evening menu. And I'll invite Doc and we'll have his favorite dessert too, apple pie. Speaking of pies, maybe I should make a few more just in case."

***

As usual, Herm and Germ had found an easy target to bully on the school ski trip. *Karilynn*! Both Josh and Mindy had tested out to be in the intermediate ski school, Dad skied with his buddies, while Germ and Herm and Karilynn joined other class mates in the beginner group. Knocked over, tripped, and even shoved off the lift, made the usual easy-going Karilynn furious. But hindered by skis, boots, and slippery snow she felt absolutely helpless.

After her third miserable ride up the lift, Ketch came swooping in on a spray of snow as the boys stood laughing over the small human snowball at the top of the lift.

"That's enough, you two are outta here!" Ketch shouted at the two boys as he stepped easily out of his skis. The Germanators, who were no match for Ketch, were de-skied and marched down the slope and introduced to the large Swiss ski school manager, Hansi, who had a thing about Germs. Both boys knew they were in deep trouble and Hansi said nothing to encourage them otherwise.

Ketch took the short lift back up to the top and found Karilynn still catching her breath on a nearby bench. She was exhausted, angry and fighting to keep tears out of her eyes. Next to her on the bench, was a stuffed bear.

"How did you know to come rescue me?" Karilynn asked, still a bit breathless. Ketch picked up the bear and tossed him into the air. "Whoooah," laughed the brown bear.

"You have interesting friends watching over you," Ketch said, as he nodded toward the woods. They both eyed the huge moose that stood watching over them from a copse of dense trees.

"You know, I do at that," declared Karilynn, "and you are fast becoming one of them."

***

84

Next morning, sitting in front of the fireplace at home, drinking marshmallow-loaded hot chocolate, the ski report began. "I can already ski blues, and I even made a few jumps," Josh proudly reported.

"A blue run is for intermediates," the solemn faced Karilynn said. "I think that Josh is going to be one of those 'hot doggers'. You know, that's a crazy person who does scary tricks…jumps off cliffs, does flips in the air…"

"Yeah, we saw films in the ski lodge while we were eating our lunch," Josh said excitedly. "They can do all kinds of tricks on skis!"

"And we can learn to race, too," Mindy's eyes gleamed. "I may not be learning as fast as Josh, but it sure is fun!"

Not exactly like water skiing that Dad taught us in Texas, but it does remind me of the good times we had on the Brazos River."

"Speaking of teaching us to water ski, Dad, wasn't that you I saw yesterday skiing with an older guy who seems to have grown up on skis? You both looked pretty experienced on those jumps for a couple of old geezers."

"Jumps and flips," Mom gasped. "Racing?" Her startled eyes frowned at Mr. Cunningham.

"Now, Sherry," Dad laughed. "It was just their first day of ski school. I don't think wild tricks are in their near future."

"Well, I don't know," Mother sighed nervously.

"Karilynn, you haven't spoken," Dad asked, changing the subject quickly. "Didn't you have a good time?"

All three children looked at each other uncomfortably.

"Well," Karilynn mumbled. Her solemn face was a hint that the day had not been a big hit with her.

"Did you fall and hurt yourself?" Mom asked worriedly.

"No, nothing like that," she said with her eyes on the floor. "It was just not the easiest day for me."

"Now, sweetheart," Dad replied naively. "You didn't expect to be a 'hot dogger' on your first day, did you?"

"Well, no," she mumbled again.

"Some of the older guys were in the beginner school, too, and when nobody was watching, they gave Karilynn a hard time," Josh blurted out.

"A hard time how?" Dad asked in stern voice. "No, you tell me, Karilynn," Dad said, as Josh opened his mouth to speak up for her.

"These two bullies have picked on all of us at school this year," she explained. "And since I was doing better than they were, they decided to push me down and stuff. But it turned out ok," she rushed on to better news, "because Ketch came along to the rescue. He turned them in to the ski school. They were sent home and lost their ski passes." Karilynn did her best to sound like that made everything all right.

"What's up with these kids?" Dad asked carefully, "Are they bugging you at school, too? What are their names?"

"Herm and John," blurted out Mindy, before thinking about the repercussions of her comment. "We call them Herm and Germ."

"Isn't that the name of those two boys who have given you so much trouble on the bus?" Dad asked.

"Yeah, and at the outdoor school, and yesterday's school ski trip," Karilynn said.

"From the first day of school when we got on the bus, they've been giving us grief," Mindy said.

"And did you do something, say something to them?" Dad asked.

"No way," Josh replied defensively. "We had just climbed aboard the stupid bus."

"Bullies," Dad murmured. "Maybe I need to go over and have a talk with some dads about their bullying sons."

"No, Dad!" All three kids reacted at once.

"We've done ok so far, Dad. I think we are in control of the situation now," Mindy spoke in her most grown up voice. That was always a good idea when trying to get Dad to change his mind about something.

"And, since the development of the "Fire-Out" teams, we've made friends with some of the older kids. Band of Brothers, (and sisters, he added when Mindy scowled at him), fighting fires together and all that stuff. I think that has made them think twice about harassing us," Josh said.

"They're right," Karilynn added. "I'm the littlest, and even I'm not afraid of them." Karilynn looked at Dad and gave him her sweetest smile. "But you can be sure that we will ask you for help if we need it," she finished, looking at Dad with her big eyes.

"Well, ok…I guess," Dad said thoughtfully.

"Good, then." Josh spoke as if it was final. The three kids grabbed their coats and hustled out the door.

Outside, the kids stomped through the deep snow away from the cabin. Hank ran around and around in circles enjoying his freedom from the house. They slid down a steep embankment, and stopped at the remains of their summer fort. Hank followed them down rolling over and over and landed at their feet. The green branches that had camouflaged the fort last summer were now dead. Loaded with new fallen snow, the fort still blended in with the white winter setting. Josh ducked inside the fort. "Don't come in," he yelled out. "It's all drippy in here." He uncovered their three canvas seats and pushed them out of the fort. "I think it's warm enough to sit outside for a few minutes."

Hank shook himself and the snow flew all over Mindy. "Now I'm all drippy," she laughed. Brushing the snow off, she sat down in her canvass chair. "This winter Colorado sun is almost warm enough to get a tan," she sighed.

"Well, I'm glad we ended up out here away from Mom and Dad," Josh said to the two girls. "This thing with Karilynn shows we have to do something. I have had a thought, a very uncomfortable thought. And since this is the site where this mystery began, this is a good place to discuss it." The girls frowned, wondering what Josh was talking about.

"Do you remember at the end of the summer when we were in here sleeping? And those three guys rode up on horseback?"

"Oh, I couldn't forget those wonderful horses," Mindy said.

"I remember," Karilynn added. "They had on dark blue uniforms and talked funny."

"Well, more important than horses and uniforms, do you remember what they said?"

"Something about a prince coming to a safe place," replied Mindy.

"I remember exactly what they said," Josh told them. He remembered everything about these unexpected visitors. Earlier in the summer, Josh had had a dangerous encounter with strangers, and now he was leery of anyone that he didn't know.

"They snuck up on our fort and woke us up. He asked us where we lived and then said, 'The prince is coming and we want to know if it's safe here.' That's what they said, and then they rode off," Josh ended his story.

"They didn't really sneak up, Josh. We were all asleep and woke up just as they arrived. I don't see any mystery here," Mindy said. "When you told Mom and Dad, they checked around and decided they were probably visiting military men from Fort Carson."

"Stop interrupting, Mindy, and let me finish," Josh snapped. "Tell me, you two, what's Herm's name?"

"Her-man," Mindy answered back sharply.

"No, no! I know that. What's his last name?"

Karilynn thought, but she didn't know. Mindy said, "It's Prince."

"That's it," Josh said. "Spelled, H-e-r-m-a-n-n P-r-i-n-z. That's not the American way to spell Herman or Prince. It's a foreign spelling. Maybe those men meant Prinz, not prince. Maybe they were talking about Herm! Maybe his dad is a foreign diplomat, or something like that."

"Ple-e-e-ze," Mindy said. "He is just a spoiled bully. Not some rich foreigner's kid."

"I don't know, Mindy," Karilynn said thoughtfully. "I've read on the internet awhile back about that evil dictator from I...Ira..."

"Iraq?" Josh asked.

"Yeah, Iraq," Karilynn went on, "who sent his sons to college here. Uniforms, soldiers. Foreign talk. It does sound like a threat, Josh. And spoiled? He is definitely a spoiled brat, and if..."

Hank, who had been racing around in the snow and running through the shallow winter stream, loped up, shook himself, and lay down between Karilynn and Mindy.

"Ok, ok," Mindy said rolling her eyes. "Maybe you two are right. What do you think, Hank?" Mindy asked the pup, as she scratched him behind his ears. His answer was a big lick on her face. Mindy laughed, swiping her face with her sleeve. "That's three votes out of four. But, so what if he is? Why would we care who he is. A bully is still a bully."

An unsettling discovery in October had once again turned the school upside down. The investigation of the fire had revealed cigarettes and matches at the point of ignition. Charred remains of homework papers had led the fire chief straight to Herm and Germ.

"Well, consider all the trouble those two have been in since the start of school. They almost burned our forest down and they're not even in jail," Josh whispered quietly. "Maybe their dad's a terrorist. They may have started that fire on purpose! Who knows what they're capable of? It could have burned our cabin down too."

"Well I know what we can do about it. We'll have *a Herm and Germ Watch Team* and ask Shannon and Ketch and a couple of others to help out." Karilynn was busy planning again. "We can call our team the Germanators, in honor of all the Germs in it."

"That's a good start," Mindy laughed along with Josh and Karilynn.

"Oh no! Another terrifying Karilynn action group," Josh said with a fearful face. And then he broke into a huge grin.

CHAPTER 11

MOUNTAIN CABIN CHRISTMAS

It was Christmas Eve and a bright Christmas moon shown through the pine trees and outlined the Magic Cabin. Two huge figures were hunkered down in the shadows of the trees just outside the cabin. Through the cabin windows, the fire in the fireplace silhouetted flames on the log walls. The Christmas tree lights blinked on and off while candles all over the cabin put on a wintery candle-glow spectacle.

The three kids burst out of the front door followed by Mom, Dad, and Doc. The quiet of the evening was shattered by the loud shouts of the family snowball fight. Everyone was slinging snowballs and dodging cold wet snow. The snow-covered kids looked like three fat snowmen. Hank ran around in circles in attack mode, knocking snow fighters to the ground.

"Brrr!! I'm heading back in," Mom laughed as she brushed the snow out of her hair! "Oh look, everybody, look!" she exclaimed. "Look at our beautiful Christmas Cabin." The family all stopped and gathered around Mom and looked.

"It *is* a Magic Christmas Cabin," Karilynn sighed as she caught her breath.

"And the best Christmas I've had in a long time," Doc said. "And with some of the best friends I've ever had." The whole group huddled together and looked at the beautiful sight.

"I'm heading in with Mom," Dad said, as he put his arm around her. Doc strode along behind them toward the cabin.

"We'll come inside in a minute," Josh spoke in a calm, clear voice. Josh quietly snuck up behind the girls and put snow down their backs.

"Yikes," they screamed as they gathered up snowballs.

"Yahoo," he yelled and started to run. A big moose stepped out in front of him. Josh slid to a stop, lost his traction, and hit the ground. Mindy and Karilynn jumped on him as soon as he fell. They threw snow all over him and bounced up and down on his stomach. When Josh pushed them off, they all lay in the snow and laughed out loud.

"Not fair," Josh shouted. "Outside interference." Hank decided to join them and he skidded up and jumped on top of all three. A wet, doggy odor surrounded them. "That's all for me," Josh puffed. "I'm going in." Everyone ran for the door. Except Hank. He ran over and snuggled down between his two moose friends, Manners and Fifty Point.

"Snack on the way," Mom said. "But first a hot shower and PJs."

In a wink, the clean, dry kids sat down around the fireplace and dug into their favorite cookies. They took small sips of Mom's gluwine. It was an old family recipe of hot red wine and spices served only at Christmas time.

"I think we should make the Cunningham Christmas Eve snowball fight a regular thing," Karilynn said.

"We could," Dad said. "We'll make it a Christmas tradition. By the way, who won the fight?"

"I did," Doc said proudly. "I had less snow on me than anybody else."

"Yes, that's true, between the six of us. But Karilynn and I won the kids snowball fight," Mindy smirked.

"You two girls beat Josh?" Mom asked, looking suspiciously at him.

"I admit, I gave in," Josh laughed. "I couldn't compete with two ferocious girls, a moose and a dog."

"Moose?" Mom looked confused.

"Uh, he meant…ah…mushy. Mushy snow did help us didn't it, Karilynn?"

"Very much so," Karilynn laughed, looking at Josh.

"I'm declaring myself the winner of tomorrow's fight. No mush is going to stop me in the daylight." Josh said, with a knowing look at the girls.

Later, Doc insisted on reading the Christmas story out of his old Bible. "That is my family's Christmas tradition." He read the whole story… angels, shepherds, sheep and inn keepers. And, of course, Mary and Joseph and the Baby Jesus.

Karilynn remembered that Doc often prayed when there were serious issues to contend with…like her broken leg last summer. She asked him hesitantly, "Doc, would you pray for our Christmas time together with Mom and Dad and you?" And with moist eyes he did just that…

***

When the grandfather clock struck eleven o'clock, orders were given to everyone to head for bed. "Did you save some of those cookies for Santa?" Doc asked.

"Santa…I guess we forgot," Mindy said. "We ate them all and left the jolly old man out!"

Sitting in Karilynn's lap, with his red vest on and his red and green plaid bow tie, BF Bear hung his head. He had a red stain around his mouth. More cookie crumbs on his fur than usual suggested that he had eaten more sweets than his share. And he had forgotten about Santa, too.

"Maybe he'll score big at other houses on the creek and won't miss the treats from our house," Josh explained, laughingly.

"You must have saved some back, didn't you, Sherry?" asked Doc.

"Well, yes, of course," she said going into the kitchen. She pulled out six cookies that she had set aside for her Christmas Day buffet of sweets. Another Christmas custom. Mrs. Cunningham always spent the weeks before Christmas baking pies, cakes, cookies and candies.

"No one in this house but me and my bear believe in Santa," Karilynn whispered in Doc's ear.

"Well, make that you *and me* and the bear," Doc smiled and brushed crumbs off of BF bear's tummy.

The house became quiet as everyone slipped off to sleep. Two large bumble bees snuck out from behind the face of the grandfather clock. They flitted from candle to candle to be sure that all had been blown out. Then the bees swooped down and buzzed around the cookies. They flew in and out of the house several times with large pieces of cookies before finally settling down outside and nestled into thick moose fur.

Above, in the guestroom, Doc was the last one to fall asleep. "Thanks Father," he uttered a sleepy prayer. "I would have had another lonely Christmas without my *sweetheart* if You hadn't brought the Cunninghams my way. He slipped into a light sleep. Much later, Doc woke up with a start. He heard bells jingling. He laid back down, rolled over with a contented smile and drifted into a deep sleep.

A few minutes later, the dog, two moose and two bees woke up with a start. Mr. and Mrs. Bee climbed up on Fifty Point's horns amid the tinsel and garlands.

A large man with a very white beard in a Christmas red suit tapped the toe of his black boots on a moose hoof. He stared at the cookie covered critters. "I see I've found my missing cookies. One cookie is a very small offering for a very large, hard working, man on Christmas Eve."

"Humph," Manners Moose grumped. "Christmas is a time of sharing, remember!"

Hank jumped up on the red-suited man and gave his hand a big lick. The man smiled, winked at the bees and stomped off through the snow.

***

Christmas Morning the kids were up early to open their Christmas surprises. First they opened their stockings.

"Shirley did a good job with the stockings," Dad thought. "But I remember agreeing we were not stuffing the stockings this year. I guess she felt Karilynn needed Santa one more year after her close call with the bear and the fire."

"Dan, you did a great job stuffing the stockings this year," Shirley said to her husband. "But I thought we had…"

"Look at Doc's cool Santa Hat everyone," Karilynn said enthusiastically, interrupting her mother's thoughts."

The authentic looking red Santa hat was decorated with hand sewn Nordic design. The white fur was some unknown material, but looked perfect with the hat. "If I didn't know better," Mrs. Cunningham thought, "I would feel like that hat fell out of Santa's sleigh as he flew over the house."

"It's a wonderful gift," Doc said with a smile, as he gave Karilynn a big wink.

After the morning festivities were over, people began to arrive for Mom's big Christmas Buffet. Grandpa, Aunt Netta and Charlie arrived first. Each one received a present from the Cunninghams. When Ketch and his grandma arrived, the children were surprised to see that the two presents left at the back of the tree were for them. "Oh, I am so glad that Dan remembered to buy them gifts," Mom thought as Ketch opened a new basketball and his grandmother oohed over her new bee-covered apron.

Between his authentic sable hat, the mysterious stocking stuffers and two presents for the guest that have no money… "It looks like Santa knew just what was needed in this house," Doc thought.

The fiesta of food was enough to fill all stomachs to the brim. "No more, thanks," Doc moaned as Mother brought out another pie.

"You ARE a wonderful cook, Sherry," said Grandpa acting surprised. He looked around the room and seemed to see the family, his family for the first time. He and Aunt Netta had given each one of the children fleece lined Jean jackets that Aunt Netta had picked out.

"Pretty great family, right Daniel?" Doc affirmed as he sat down next to his old friend. Grandpa just stared at the Santa hat on Doc's head, and then glared at him.

"Go ahead and frown at me all you want, because they are going to win you over. I guess you think I don't know that you snuck into Karilynn's hospital room with one of those beautiful blooming cactus plants after her wrestling match with that bear. Dug it right up yourself and then spent money on a pot to put it in. As soon as I saw it, I knew that you were the mystery gift giver. I think Karilynn liked it better than all the other flowers, because she loved having a secret admirer."

Grandpa mumbled out loud, got up, and moved across the room. "You can run, but you can't hide!" Doc shouted after him, with a big smile on his face. Doc glanced upward and silently prayed…"My Christmas wish is that he'll quit hiding when the kids come around his ranch!"

***

Christmas Day ended with a huge snowball fight at Monte Vista school and as many sled rides as one could hope for. Half the school attended the Christmas Day festivities, and Mr. Smoklin used the school's bulldozer to create a long and winding sled run.

Winter darkness set in at five o'clock and Karilynn, Josh, and Mindy headed back home with cold toes and noses. They sat down next to the warm fireplace, while Mom and Dad served cookies and hot chocolate. Later they had a meal of turkey leftovers. "Man, I never get tired of turkey," Josh said.

"Me either," chimed in Karilynn, "and I have something I would like to say, even if it isn't New Years Eve." Her family looked curiously at her as she straightened up and cleared her throat.

"I know we have a tradition on New Year's Eve to say what we are most thankful for about the past year. I can't wait a whole week to say it. I'm just bursting with smiles inside of me wanting to say, 'This is my best year ever.' Doc, and our other new friends," she went on, winking at her brother and sister. "And our adventures and..."

"We get it, Sis," Josh said giving her a big smile. "But do save a little for New Years Eve!"

"Here, here," Dad said, raising his hot chocolate toward his smiling daughter. Mom and Josh joined in. Mom was quietly keeping her eye on Mindy.

She was looking at her Christmas cup and you could sense her realization that they would never return to their Texas home. The move to Colorado had been hardest on her, and after getting over feeling sorry for herself, she had really tried to grab hold of Colorado.

Hank, BF Bear, the bumble bees, Manners and Fifty Point, streamed across her mind. The forest fire and Fire-Out friends she had made continued the stream of thoughts. Charlie, the horses, Hi-Lonesome Ranch, and meeting her new best friend, Shannon, tipped the scale in her mind that their new Colorado home was worth all she had given up in Texas.

All of a sudden Mindy noticed that it was very quiet and each one of her family was waiting with their cup in the air. "Here, here," she said, "I'll drink to that," and raised her cup to her family.

CHAPTER 12

A NEW FRIEND

Soon the spring term was underway but the high country snows kept on falling. "It's always like this, Mindy. The snowiest months in Colorado are March and April." Shannon was giving Mindy some advanced ski tips on the slopes. Shannon, who was a typical Colorado born skier, headed straight down the blue slope and stopped at the next flat spot on the ski run.

"Turn Mindy, turn," she yelled to Mindy where she had left her. Start now! Good job…ok, start again. Turn…Mindy. Stop… dig your skis in and STOP NOW!"

Mindy was standing right over her skis. They were side by side running down hill. Mindy's arms were wind milling as she tried to get in control.

"Uh oh," thought Shannon. She is heading right for that stand of trees. "Fall down Mindy, to stop yourself…F-A-L-L D-O-W-N N-O-W!!!" she hollered louder.

"At least I can do that," Mindy thought. She plopped down right on the slope, but began sliding down the steep hill, losing her poles as she went. Finally she stopped when she slid into Shannon who has skied over to the trees to keep her from sliding into the forest.

Shannon landed right on top of her, but she had skillfully stepped out of her ski's knowing that Mindy was coming her way. She laughed out loud and rolled off of Mindy who was trying to control her tears.

"Dang nabitt," Mindy moaned. "This is 100 times harder than learning to ride a horse. I quit!"

"Oh no you're not, my flatlander friend! This is the hardest year. Every skier has to go through it. By next year you'll be zooming down the slopes and thinking, 'This is a piece of cake. I love it!'"

"Sure. That's easy for you to say. You've been skiing since you were six years old."

"True, but most people don't start at six!" Shannon gave her a hand up, and sidestepped skillfully up the hill to recover her ski poles.

"Shannon, I'm all wet and freezing. Is this really what you guys call warm Spring Skiing?" Mindy asked while chattering.

"I'm not listening to any more whining. And I am *not* going to help you get your skis on. That'll warm you up, and we *are* going to climb back on the horse and ski down to the lodge. I'll buy you a hot chocolate with my meager allowance!"

Soon they joined up with a smiling Karilynn and Josh! They had loved their day of skiing! "I got thrown off my horse more times than I can count, but I'm just going to love this skiing stuff," Mindy said through gritted teeth.

***

Three weeks later on a bright, warm and sunny Saturday, Mindy was hiding a secret smile as Josh moaned that all the ski slopes had closed the week before and there would be no more skiing until next winter. "We'll still have more snow," grumbled Josh, "but they always close the runs the second week of April."

"I'm gonna head over to Hi-Lonesome if you'll give me a ride, Dad." Mindy asked.

"I'd be glad to take you, Mindy. And while I'm at it, I can drop Josh off in Monte Vista to find a game of pick-up basketball... and you can visit some of your friends, Karilynn." That cheered up everyone.

When Dad dropped off Mindy at the ranch, she ran straight into the barn. Charlie was mending tack while a teenage boy had the saddle soap and was wiping down a saddle.

"Hello," Mindy said taking in the boy's long black hair and dark eyes. "Who are you?"

"Oh, let me introduce you," Charlie said, as he came back from the tack room. "Mindy, this is Tomás (pronounced toe-mas), and Tomás, this is my good friend Mindy. Look, this is how we do it here. Stick out your hand and give hers a shake." Charlie grabbed Mindy's hand and shook it. Then he put her hand in Tomás's and had them shake.

"Tomás is here at the Hi-Lonesome Ranch to learn English and how to train and care for horses."

"Oh," Mindy smiled at the quiet, shy boy.

"There's your saddle, girl, and some Neatsfoot Oil. Work on your saddle first and then you can teach Tomás how to muck out the stalls."

Mindy found her saddle, set it up on a saw horse and went to work. After an hour's work, Mindy hollered out at Charlie, "We're through in here."

"You just got here Mindy, but we've been at it a long time; so I'm calling a break." Charlie gave her a shove toward the house. Tomás's eyes got big as he watched them shove back and forth, but he said nothing and headed up to the house.

"Sit down and I'll bring you some hot chocolate for your morning break," Aunt Netta said. It was still too chilly to sit outside, so Mindy took her coat off in the warm kitchen. They sat down at the wooden table and dug into the pile of biscuits that Aunt Netta placed on the table along side cups of frothy chocolate.

All but Tomás, who sat still with his hands in his lap, waiting for something. "What's he waiting for," Mindy wondered. "Here," she said, and pushed the plate closer to him. "Dig in!"

Tomás looked over at Charlie, and he nodded for Tomás to go ahead. Tomás stretched out his hand, took a bite, and gave Aunt Netta a huge smile.

"Ah, you like them?" she asked.

"Yes, all of your food is good, but I think I like your biscuits the best," replied Tomás, with a big grin on his face.

"You're a good eater, Tomás" Aunt Netta said.

Charlie laughed. "And that's what keeps you happy… right Netta?"

"Right," Aunt Netta said, "and clean kitchens, clean rooms, clean kids…"

"We got it," Mindy said laughing. "*Clean* is your favorite word." Then there was no more talking in the room, just the crunching and slurping sounds of happy snackers.

Finally, Charlie leaned back with a smile. "Well, back to work," he said after they were warm and full. He slid back his chair and nodded Aunt Netta a thanks.

Tomás headed for the door, then stopped short, turned and said politely, "Thank you for the food."

"Yeah, thanks Aunt Netta," Mindy hollered back over her shoulder as they ran out the door together.

"And polite kids!" Netta thought to herself. "I like polite kids...don't know what's happened to them...not many around... so I'm glad that Tomás is learning good manners."

"Stall mucking 101," Mindy said to herself. She got out two stiff brooms and shovels to clean out the stalls. "My least favorite part of horses. I won't tell Tomás that. Maybe Charlie will give him this job and I won't have to do it every time I'm here." She smiled at the thought.

They cleaned the first stall together. Tomás was a quick learner, but then, mucking was not a hard job to learn, just a stinky one.

Mindy was surprised that he walked right into the stalls seemingly unafraid of hooves or teeth. Both of them working together had the job done in half the time it took Mindy.

"This is the part I like best," Mindy told Tomás. She climbed up to the loft and knocked down some of the fresh hay bales. Climbing down she said, "Now, we take the fresh hay and spread it around in the stalls."

"Much or little?" Tomás asked.

Watching her, he started to help with the other stalls. Mindy threw him the water hose, and said, "Fill up each trough with fresh water." She ran to turn on the hose and Tomás carefully filled the troughs. He did not want to splash water on the fresh hay.

"Great!" she said, taking a deep breath and smelling the new clean hay.

"What's up there...hay? Can I see up there?" asked Tomás, climbing up into the hayloft.

"That's all that's up there, Tomás. We're feeding them oats right now until the weather warms up and the hays ready to cut. Oats are down here in the bin."

Tomás ran to the end of the loft and looked down. "Wow," Tomás said, using the new expression that Charlie had taught him.

"You've had some poor English teachers," Charlie thought, with a frown, at some of the English exclamations that Tomás used.

"That's a huge pile of goats," Tomás shouted and leaped into the bin!"

"No, don't do that," Mindy tried to shout before he jumped. Tomás fought his way to the top of the pile, reached out and drug Mindy in.

"N-o-o!" Mindy exclaimed. He pushed her under the mountain of oats. She came up irritably blowing oats out of her nose and spitting them out or her mouth.

"I'm sorry," Tomás said with a flustered look on his face. "I have seen you and Charlie laughing and boxing. I do that with my own sisters; so I was just boxing with you."

"I'm not angry," she laughed, "but I gotta teach you three things. First, you are not boxing with me, nor fighting...it's called teasing. Second, this feed is not called goats...that's an animal... it's called oats!"

"Oats, not goats," Tomás mumbled to himself. "Not fighting, but tee-sing," he said. "That is two things. What is the third? he asked holding up the last of three fingers.

"Playing in oats makes you itch all over!!" Mindy caught him off guard and shoved him back into the oats. He thrashed his way back to the top. Mindy was waiting with hands full of more grain to throw in his face and down his back.

"Stop," he pleaded, and jump from the oats to the concrete floor. "What does this itching mean?"

Mindy began to scratch her arm.

"Oh…" he said as he began to itch, too. They spit oats out of their mouths while stomping their feet with more oats falling out of their clothes. Both shook their heads. Oats were dropping from everywhere, and the end did not seem in sight.

"I can't handle this the rest of the day," Mindy said. "I'm heading up to the house to clean up and change clothes. Why don't you head over to the bunkhouse and wash up! Don't worry about Charlie. I'll explain it all to him later."

When Mindy returned to the barn, Charlie was showing Tomás a booklet on training horses in a ring. Tomás had never seen a Horse Training Ring before and was fascinated by the whole process.

"Once you finished reading this, I'll loan you one called the Horse Whisperer. It's basically our bible on training mustangs," Charlie shared with both kids. "Anyone who trains horses for a living has memorized this book."

Charlie handed both kids a small paperback folder entitled, "Training Horses the Proper Way" by Red Rider.

Both kids gathered around the pamphlet and looked over the info and pictures on the proper training of horses. Several suggestions seemed to stick out clearly.

1. *All wild horses are ingrained by nature with the fear and flight response. When they're afraid, they take off. Not much stops a 1500 pound horse in full stride.*

2. *Training must be safe for the trainer and the horse. An unfenced training area is looking for a ride to the hospital.*

3. *Develop trust with your horse to replace his fear. It heightens both horse and rider confidence. Talk to him, pat on him, rub his neck, back and withers, etc.*

4. *Reward good behavior with a handful of grain or some apple slices. Some trainers prefer you feed the horse its treat from a small bucket.*

5. *Horses get bored by repetitious teaching techniques. After a new lesson, go back over lessons the horse has already mastered to build confidence.*

6. *Introduce your horse to the blanket and saddle gradually. Show it to him at first and then walk around him carrying the blanket. Be sure and unfold the blanket slowly, as a flapping blanket will scare off any critter. Rub the horse with the blanket also to let him get used to it.*

7. *Then, take your saddle and sit it on the horses back. Put it on and take it off several times. Then bounce the saddle while putting it on, letting the stirrups bounce off the horse a few times. Let the horse run around the ring with his blanket and saddle on to teach him he can't get rid of them.*

8. *The horse should be calmer after the lesson than before, otherwise you're doing something wrong.*

"There's some good ideas here, Charlie," Mindy said while continuing to read along with Tomás. "Sounds like you wrote this booklet."

"Nah, I just memorized it years ago and have passed it along to several generations of new riders and now…you two."

"Isn't it about time for your mom to pick you up, Mindy?" asked Charlie wisely. "You know she doesn't like to wait around too long. Might already be in the kitchen chatting with Netta."

"I'll go and check, see you guys later."

CHAPTER 13

THE SECRET GIFT

Mindy was back at Hi-Lonesome the next weekend. After helping Tomás with his daily chores, they headed into the barn for their morning break. Aunt Netta had gone to town, so they were having Charlie's Tea. It was jerky...thinly sliced meat that was smoked and cured. After a lot of Charlie's Tea... that's what Mindy had named it...she had learned to enjoy the tough-to-eat jerky. Today's tea included jerky, brown bread he had snatched from Netta's kitchen, and a thermos full of strong coffee. Mindy looked at the dark coffee and reached for her water bottle.

"What's next?" Tomás asked Charlie, after waiting hopefully for a chocolate chip cookie to appear. "I guess cookies aren't a part of Charlie's Tea," he thought to himself. He caught Mindy's twinkling eyes laughing at him.

"I want you two to take these fencing tools out to Rip who is working on that ten acres down by the creek. I saw the truck go by to deliver the wire to him, and I noticed that he left these here. He'll be ready for them soon enough." Charlie split the tools into saddle bags for each horse.

"Are you sure that Tomás can ride that horse?" Mindy asked with worried eyes. Charlie had picked out Trail Blazer for Tomás to ride. He was a beautiful grey-spotted gelding.

"Hmmm," Charlie nodded his head to answer the question. "You told me you're bored riding the horses I've had you on," Charlie said to Tomás. "Mind what you're doing and he'll be a great ride."

After they had saddled up the horses, Charlie helped them with the heavy saddlebags, and sent them on their way.

Mindy started off slowly looking warily at Tomás on his horse.

"You ride good for a girl," Tomás said teasingly. "I think we should trot a little."

"I've ridden Lady a lot," she said, "but you're a new rider on a new horse. Just loosen the reigns in your hands, and he'll walk faster. But no trotting!"

Twenty-five slow minutes later, they found Rip using the post hole digger and putting in the last new post. "Thanks," he said with a big smile. "Now I can work right on through the afternoon and not stop for my usual nap."

When they left, Mindy said. "Lady and I want to take you and Trail Blazer to one of our favorite spots on the Hi-Lonesome Ranch. It's not too far from here, so we can go up there and still get back for afternoon chores."

"And snack," Tomás said.

The spring runoff had turned the creek into a roaring stream. They followed it until they came to a crossing. The water changed directions and that left a shallow crossing to the other side. Once across, Mindy rode off away from the stream, and through a small meadow.

"Do you hear that?" she asked

"How can I not hear that? What is it?"

"Come on, I'll show you." Mindy started off at a trot, and Tomás followed her through the meadow. She continued on until they again came to the stream. They had been climbing out of the meadow, and when they stopped, there was a beautiful water fall splashing down over the big rocks below them.

"Wow!" Tomás said. He looked in amazement at the high falls that were making the loud noise in the meadow.

"Isn't it awesome," Mindy said with a huge smile.

"Awesome," thought Tomás, testing the new word in his mouth.

"Let's tie the horses up and enjoy the falls for a bit."

Both kids climbed out of the saddle, and Mindy showed Tomás how to tie the horses securely to the trees. He was a quick learner and did not need much help to get it right. The reigns lagged and the horses happily munched on the new spring grass.

Mindy took a hidden deer trail up along side of the big rocks. They climbed upward for ten minutes, and then she stopped and turned around to Tomás with a big smile on her face.

"Now, raise your right hand," Mindy instructed. She raised her own hand, and he did the same. Do you know what an oath is?"

Tomás shook his head. "It's like a special promise that you give to another person," she explained.

"Like a special promise you make to get married?" he asked doubtfully looking her straight in the eyes.

Mindy blushed a deep red. "No! No way! Well, never mind. Just raise your right hand and say this."

"My hand is up," Tomás pointed out.

"I promise I will never, never, never show or tell anyone about this secret place."

Tomás started out saying, "I will not never, not never tell anyone about this secret place."

They both smiled and Mindy started again picking her way over large boulders that lay very close to the water fall. The boulders were slick from the spray of the falls. "Be careful," Mindy shouted back over her shoulder. "It's very slick along here."

Tomás, looking down at his feet, carefully climbed the boulders. When he looked up, Mindy was not in sight. He looked at the higher boulders, down on the ground, everywhere that he could see. And still no Mindy. "I wonder where could she be?" he asked himself.

Like a ghost she popped into his line of vision. Hidden in a deep mist, her hand was waving for him to come on up. When he finally reached her she grabbed his hand and they squeezed between two tall boulders. A few more steps and they were high and dry right under the falls.

The loud noise that had filled his ears before had become a quieter sound more like a rushing stream. He looked up towards the falls and saw the rushing water resembling diamonds dancing down to the next level.

"This is it, The Secret Place." Mindy twirled around with her arms out, showing off the secret cave under the water falls.

"Awesome!" Tomás remembered that word, and used it to explain how he felt about the waterfall cave. "How did you ever find this place?"

"Charlie, of course," she said with a smile. "It's his secret place, and he told me I could show it to you."

Both kids were wringing wet and shivering, but had not noticed until they had finally stopped gaping at the beauty. "Brrr, I'm freezing!" Mindy said. "And your face is turning blue. Look here." Mindy walked to a dark corner of the cave and pulled back a large plastic sheet. She opened up an old wooden trunk and grabbed Tomás a dry sweatshirt and socks. Another trunk sat close by, with a big stack of wood and two bedrolls."

With backs turned, the kids pulled off their wet coats and shirts and pulled on the dry sweatshirts. Sitting on the floor of the cave to change socks, Mindy said, "It's perfect in here in the summer. If it gets a little cold, you can build a fire to warm up."

"Could we do that now?" Tomás asked, looking hopeful.

"Nope, I promised Charlie that we would come back to the ranch and help with the chores. Stretch your wet things here, and if you stay for part of the summer we can come back and have a picnic or something."

Tomás watched as Mindy wrung the water from her jacket, and tied it around her waist. She placed the other wet things flat on the old trunk.

Following suit, he did the same, but didn't walk out with Mindy. He stayed to look at the wonderful Secret that Charlie and Mindy had shared with him. When he finally squeezed through the two rocks, he caught sight of Mindy almost down to where they had tied the horses. It took him awhile, but he finally caught up with her.

"Thought I'd have to come back up and rescue you."

"Well…"

"I know," she finished his thought. "Its hard for me to leave every time too. But we've gotta move on towards home." The afternoon sun was warming their chilled clothes as they climbed up on Trail Blazer and Lady. "Did you feel comfortable trotting when we came through the valley?"

"Yes," he replied with a small smile. "Let's go."

"All right, we'll trot, but watch Trail Blazer. Horses get excited when they know they're heading to the barn. Don't give him his head. Let him know you're the boss," she ordered. "I still can't figure out why Charlie put a rookie up on one of the more spirited horses at the ranch," she mumbled under her breath.

Both horses trotted along, but when Lady came to the stream where they had crossed before, a mountain goat jumped out of the bushes. Lady, startled by the animal, reared up and bucked. "Whoa, whoa," Mindy said strongly, but one more buck and she was thrown off the horse and landed hard in the thistle bushes on the edge of the stream.

Tomás slid off his horse, and rushed to Mindy.

"I'm all right" she said rather embarrassed. "Give me a sec and I'll get back on Lady."

"No, you are hurt," Tomás spoke firmly. He eyed the blood covering her head and he gently pulled her out of the bushes and laid her down by the stream. "You are not going anywhere. Let me take a look." He parted her hair in several places, noticing that the blood was still seeping out.

Tomás quickly unsaddled his horse, and pulled off the saddle blanket. He folded it over and put it under Mindy's head. After unsaddling Lady, he laid her blanket and their partly dried jackets over Mindy. Then he tied Lady's reigns loosely around her neck.

He unsheathed a knife that was pushed into his boot, and handed it to her. "What's that for?" she asked.

"I do not know, but it seems like the right idea," he answered. "But, do not go to sleep. I think you might have a…a…what do you call it? A broken head?" Tomás took a few fast steps and leaped onto Trail Blazer's back.

"Remember, don't go to sleep," he said to Mindy before he started off. "I'll be back in 25 minutes."

Tomás nudged the horse, and they took off running. Mindy leaned up on her elbow. "Where did he learn to ride like that," her confused brain wondered. The pain returned and forced her back down on the blanket. Her head was throbbing with pain. She just wanted to sleep, but she heard Tomás's strong warning…"Do not go to sleep!"

Charlie was outside the barn when he looked up and saw a rider running full out. Seeing Tomás's long black hair blowing around his head, his heart leaped into his throat. Lady was right behind him, but without a rider.

In less than a minute, Tomás had explained what had happened and where Mindy was along the creek. "I think she has a broken head."

"Concussion," Charlie said unthinkingly. "Wait here." He ran to the barn and came out with a bedroll. Throwing it to Tomás, he said, "Get back to her right now. I'll get the pickup and come find you." In a split second Charlie unharnessed Lady, had her in the corral, and rushed toward the pickup.

When Tomás rode up to the creek, he slid off Trail Blazer and, grabbing the bedroll, completely wrapped Mindy from head to toe. Only her head stuck out, and she said through chattering teeth, "I didn't go to sleep, Tomás, I was too cold." Tomás didn't reply but was gently looking at her bloody head. Mindy grimaced but then a thought flashed through her mind. "How the heck did you ride Trail Blazer like that? I thought you were just learning how to ride?" Knowing how bad she felt, he still didn't miss the anger flash through her eyes.

"Be quiet mi querida," he said gently. "Charlie will be here soon." He brushed his tears away with his shirtsleeve. And sure enough, a few minutes later, Charlie came wheeling into the clearing.

He knelt beside her, looking at her head. He found a huge egg shaped bump under her hair. "I wonder about her legs and arms?" he said talking to himself. He drew the bedroll back and poked around finding nothing serious. "Can you stand up, Mindy?"

"I think so," she said. "The only thing wrong with me is I'm cold. I don't know why Tomás wouldn't let me mount up. I'm embarrassed that I lost my seat and went flying off Lady like a beginner. And did you know that Tomás, the liar, can ride like the wind? I want to punch him in the..."

"Mindy, hush!" Charlie said, breaking into her ranting. "Save all of your strength so we can get you into the nice warm pick up."

Charlie stood her up gently, putting one arm around Tomás' shoulder. He slipped her other arm around his shoulder and they walked slowly to the pickup. "Ah, warm," she murmured as Charlie lifted her into the pickup and wrapped her in a blanket.

"Tomás, ride to the ranch and get Netta to call her folks. We'll be at the Monte Vista Clinic."

Saying that, Charlie roared off toward town. Tomás stood, looking forlornly after his friends.

CHAPTER 14

MINDY'S PRISON

"Oh no!" Mindy looked at the doctor. "No horseback riding…
For a month?" Mindy looked pleadingly at the clinic doctor. She
was surrounded by Charlie and her mom and dad.

After several test, the doctor had explained the CT scan. His
verdict was that Mindy only had a slight concussion, but she must
take precautions for at least a month.

"My brother told me that NFL players with concussions can
start getting knocked around again in their games after two
weeks."

"You're not an NFL player," the doctor said laughingly, "and
even though it is just a slight concussion, you need to be extra
careful about your head. And I said…*if you progress as I hope you
will*…you can ride again in a month."

Mindy would never have admitted it, but she soon found out that she did not feel like riding for the first two week. With dizziness and headaches, she was pushing herself to go to school and get her homework done.

One day when Tomás was keeping her company at her house, Mindy had a sudden memory. "Tomás, I thought you couldn't ride a horse. You said you were here to learn to ride. When I fell…I may have been groggy…but I didn't miss you leaping up on Trail Blazer. And with no saddle…you raced off and returned before I could hardly blink." Mindy's eyes were dark with fire.

"I did not say I could not ride a horse. I said I was here to learn to care for horses…you know, curry, muck, feed, that kind of stuff."

"What?" Mindy asked louder and grumpier than she meant to. "You can ride like that, but you don't know how to take care of a horse?" Her head was hurting, but she didn't like it one bit that Tomás was holding out on her.

"You are not going to believe what I am about to tell you," he said with a grimace. "But I will try to explain." His face broke into a big smile. "But first you have to put up your right hand and take an oath…like I did at the water fall."

Mindy looked confused.

"Raise your right hand," he said, putting his in the air. "And promise you will never, never, *never* tell anyone about me."

***

Gradually the symptoms faded and she was ready to be at Hi-Lonesome again. Although the doctor said she could hang out with Charlie and Tomás, she still had to wait until the month was over before she could ride again. "The beginning of summer will be a good time," the doctor instructed.

Sitting in the loft, Mindy was so glad to be back at the ranch. "You do all the work," Mindy teased one day while she was watching Tomás muck stalls. "So maybe being on "Doctor's Watch" is not such a bad deal after all."

"Yes, but don't forget I get to ride everyday."

"Yeah, you do get the fun stuff, too," she said with a gloomy face.

"Oops," Tomás thought when he saw her sad face. "I guess I should not have said that." He decided to change the subject.

"Did you hear about our Mustang Roundup? I get to choose a wild mustang to be my own horse. I'll train him and everything."

"No, I haven't heard anything about that," Mindy seemed even gloomier than before.

"Oops! I should not have said anything," he thought to himself.

"I guess Charlie has not wanted to mention it because you can not ride yet. But we are not going without you. Charlie promised me."

"Really?" Mindy asked, her face brightening. "Let's go talk to him right now."

They found Charlie in the old log barn checking the feed that was stored there. "Charlie," Mindy exclaimed as she raced into the barn. "Why haven't you told me anything about a Mustang Roundup?"

"What Roundup?" he asked, looking at Tomás with a frown.

Tomás hung his head. "I think I spilled the beans out of the pot."

"Yes, you did spill the beans…not out of the pot, but into my ears.

"Come on, Charlie, what's up? Can I go, too?" Mindy found herself worrying that they might not let her go. Of course, Tomás being an expert horseman, would get to go.

"All right, all right, little girl. Settle down. Of course you're going. Let's go in for a break. I think Aunt Netta has tea for us."

Going in the big kitchen they found milk, tea, and Texas chocolate sheet cake sitting on the round table. The cake was hot and gooey, fresh out of the oven.

"Now, don't ya'll even think about eating all of that cake," warned Aunt Netta. "Cut one large piece for each of you, and leave the rest. I have to take part of it to the school concert tonight."

Charlie gave each kid a big piece, as well as himself. "What's going on with the three of you?" Aunt Netta asked. "Mindy, you're looking a lot perkier than a few days ago."

"I just heard about the Mustang Roundup!" she replied, with an even bigger smile.

"Well," Charlie said slyly. "It's not going to be too exciting. First we camp out, then we round up eight mustangs and herd them to Hi-Lonesome. Then we train one for you and one for Tomás and the others we'll get ready for adoption."

Mindy's eyes grew bigger and bigger. "We can't do all that!" Mindy exclaimed.

"Charlie says we can," smiled Tomás.

"Well, of course we can. You, me, your grandpa, Tomás, and Rip and Sam," Charlie counted off on his fingers. "The six of us will be plenty to do the cowboying. Camping gear, food, a couple of extra horses. We'll be there and back in five days, six at the most."

Quiet fell on the group around the kitchen table. Charlie and Tomás sat smiling, munching on their cake and slurping their milk.

Mindy's mind was whirling with questions. "Mom and Dad won't let me go, will they? Where will we camp? What will we eat? How do we get the horses we want, or do we just take the first eight we find? How do we get home? Drive them down highways?" She ate her cake, but her thoughts were swirling so fast that she didn't even taste it… quite strange since Texas chocolate sheet cake was one of her favorites.

"Do you think Mom and Dad will let me go?"

"You'll never know until you ask them? So how bout you head on home and find out," suggested Aunt Netta.

Dinner that night was buzzing with Mustang conversation. Mindy had explained all the things they would be doing. Mother had a big frown on her face.

Josh was barely listening as he didn't care about horses or ranch life. He did like his Mom's cooking and his focus was on food.

"You can't just go out and capture mustangs and bring them home. They are protected by the U.S. government's *Wild Horse Rules* and *Regulations*. Even adopting a Mustang is a serious process. I read about them on my computer for a class report," Karilynn lectured in her teacher's voice.

"If the government's involved, it'll never happen. Too much paperwork," Josh said.

Mother's face brighten a little with the impossibilities of the possibilities.

"Don't you kids know your grandpa better than to worry about a little thing like paperwork?" Mr. Cunningham asked, with a wink at Mindy. Her face was changing from excitement to gloom as the conversation bounced back and forth.

"Dan, what do you know about all this? Have you and Charlie been talking behind my back?" questioned Mrs. Cunningham.

"Mindy could be killed by those wild horses. Or thrown in jail for breaking the law by chasing wild mustangs. *No! Its just not going to happen*," Mom said, emphasizing each word. Her stern face glowered at her husband

"You kids, scat and do your homework." Dad said "You, too, Mindy. Mom and I'll discuss this and give you our decision later." He winked again and shooed the kids out of the room with his hand.

"Now Mother! They'll get government permission…Grandpa's done this many…Charlie will be there… be an Adventure of a life time…and you love for your kids to have adventures."

All Mindy could hear were snippets of her Dad's argument, and her mother continually saying only one word. "NO!"

But an hour later Dad came into her room…"Mom's essentially agreed!"

***

As we all know, it seems like the end of school will never come. Now Mindy not only had riding again to look forward to, but the Mustang hunt. It was all she could do to keep her mind on her school work. She had to make herself concentrate as she feared that bad grades would lead to summer school, and then, no Roundup would be a part of her summer. Not only did she have to do her regular school work, but make sure that the work she had been unable to do while sick was all up to date.

Of course, Mindy's grades were never an issue, and Summer School was not in her future. But the good thing about all her worrying was, it gave her the extra push to get all her homework caught up.

***

It wasn't too long before the final bell rang, and all of the students cheered and headed for the doors. Outside, the enthusiasm swirled around the kids and even the air seemed filled with anticipation.

They chatted with friends and talked over summer plans. Josh was going to Tugboat's Football Camp every day in June.

Karilynn was going to a new camp called The Idea Camp... or TIC for short. She would be gone for two weeks. They would be online with their computers to research new and creative ideas that each child would present to the group. They had planned excursions woven into the program, to take their creative ideas on the road. Karilynn's was, of course, forest fires. Another child wanted to study Wind Farms.

All Mindy could think about was getting out to Grandpa's to ride and get ready for the Mustang Roundup. She and Shannon ran out the door together screaming with excitement. Days ago Shannon had been "included" in the Mustang Roundup. Horse-loving girlfriends jumped around as they talked on top of one another about the upcoming Mustang adventure.

At dinner that night, Mom and Dad presented the Summer Cabin Restoration Plan. They had given each kid their jobs and chores worked into a schedule that would allow them each to have the month of June off. But then the family would gather together in July to continue making their rustic log cabin into a home.

The expected groans did not show up. They received their assigned lists with cheerful smiles. Mom and Dad looked at each other with puzzlement on their faces. The children all thought the same thing...July is a long way off!

***

The next day found Josh and Karilynn happily sleeping in on the first day of summer break. Mom and Dad were still tucked into their beds enjoying a quiet morning of coffee and tea. Mindy came into their room to wave goodbye. "I called Charlie and he said that he had time to come pick me up. It's my first day to ride again!" Mindy was smiling from ear to ear.

"Great," said Dad as he raised his coffee mug in a salute towards Mindy.

"Now, Mindy," Mom said, sitting up in bed. "You must start slowly. It will be like learning to ride again since you haven't ridden in such a long time. And…"

"You have a great day, Mindy," Dad said, patting Mom on the hand.

And she did. Charlie let her saddle up right away, and she rode for two hours with Tomás. She was a little sore when she hopped off Lady, but she jumped right in to help Tomás with the chores.

There were snacks before lunch followed by a meeting with Grandpa and Charlie about the Mustang Roundup.

"Tomás," Grandpa said in a serious voice. "This is a momentous day at the Hi-Lonesome Ranch." Tomás' usual lively face was solemn and he straightened up as tall as he could in his chair.

You are the fourth Prince from Maracabito to come and seek an American Mustang. Your great grandfather came to Hi-Lonesome before I was born. He had read about the wild horses in books and heard stories of the western frontier from his far away cousins in Estados Unidos.

Then your grandpa came when I was still a teenager. Grandpa's eyes looked out the window and he seemed to have drifted away. What he was remembering was the handsome young prince, only a few years older than himself when they first met. Señor Tomás Castillo had explained to him all of the stories he had heard growing up about the Wild Mustang Horses in Western American. He longed to hunt them and choose a Black Stallion for his own, just like his father had. It would be a great honor for The Mustangs, and he confided, a real victory for himself. He had fought a lengthy battle with his parents to receive this as his "right of passage into manhood." They had both laughed together when he told the story.

"You look just like your grandfather, Tomás, and you ride a lot like him...fast and furious," Grandpa said, as he brought his mind back into the present. "However, six guardianes came with him to give him the protection that he needed back in the day." Grandpa gave a small laugh. "When it was your father's time to come, he refused to bring along the guardianes and he came alone. And here you are as well, all alone. We feel so honored to have yet one more generation of the Castillo family ride with us on our Mustang Roundup."

CHAPTER 15

THE MUSTANG TRAIL

By the time Grandpa finished his speech, the entire group was in tears...especially Tomás.

Tomás made a slight bow to Grandpa. "Thank you, sir. I am honored to live at your ranch, and to learn from Mr. Charlie and your granddaughter how to care for horses. I look forward to the roundup and appreciate your hospitality by allowing me to go on this adventure." Grandpa nodded his head to Tomás.

He slowly turned to Mindy, "Now, as for you, Mindy, you can win those spurs hanging on the wall over there if you round up your own mustang and train him yourself. They first belonged to your great grandmother, Mindy Lou, when she captured and broke her mustang. No one on the ranch thought that she could do that. Your great grandfather had the spurs made for Mindy Lou as her trophy."

"Here is a picture of her with those spurs, and this is a picture of when she presented them to your grandmother, my sweet Ellie." Grandfather said, with tears in his eyes, as he handed her the two framed photos that normally hung on either side of the spurs.

Her great grandmother was dressed in a leather fringed skirt, white blouse with big puffy sleeves, and a leather fringed vest. She was slender with long hair. Mindy caught her breath in surprise. She felt like she was looking at herself in a mirror. Her great grandmother stood with her hip cocked to the left, and had a huge smile on her face. She looked full of confidence as she held the spurs in her hands.

In the next photo was the lady Mindy had never met. "My beautiful grandmother Ellie that married my grumpy ol' grandpa," she marveled, wondering what she saw in him.

She was a handsome lady who looked a lot like Mindy's Dad. Great Grandmother Cunningham and her daughter smiled at each other with loving eyes and obvious affection.

"I haven't figured out who should present them to you if you actually catch and train a mustang," Grandpa said thoughtfully. "But they will be yours to keep until one of your kin captures and trains her own horse."

Mindy gasped…she couldn't speak. She had never heard a kind word from him, and had always thought of him as the Grumpy Grandfather. Now this same grandfather was offering her these historic spurs, which obviously meant so much to him.

Finally, Mindy found her voice. "Grandfather," she addressed him formally. "I really want to try and catch that mustang…and I think I can do it. And if I do, I promise to take good care of your treasured spurs."

"Our family's spurs," Grandpa corrected quietly, looking down at the floor. "We'll see what happens on the roundup."

***

The Cunningham Summer Adventures started the second week of June. Karilynn was off to Camp TIC and Josh was staying in town with a buddy to attend Tugboat's Football Camp.

As Karilynn had continued to do more research on wild fires, she had taken time off to learn more about Mustangs so Mindy could be informed. She produced what she thought was a useful booklet with the history of the American Mustang and where their grazing lands are today.

Mindy was not interested in the booklet until she saw what a great effort Karilynn was putting into it. "Why don't you paint pictures of the horses?" Karilynn asked her sister.

And she did just that. Mindy had not painted since before the fire. She got out her paints and canvasses and started sketching out Mustangs. Any time she was not at the ranch, she was sketching and painting.

One night the family sat around the table to learn more about Mustangs. Mother had insisted that the family should be involved in what the girls were doing. Charlie, Doc, and Tomás joined them for a dinner of fried chicken, mashed potatoes and gravy, and blueberry cobbler for desert.

After dinner Karilynn handed around copies of her Mustang Booklet so each one could read along.

> *"Horses were first brought to our continent by the conquistadors from Spain. Many escaped from these men or were stolen by American Indians. They also escaped from pioneer ranches and farms, or were let go when people gave up homesteading and moved back east."*

Tomás gave Karilynn his full attention, while Josh got up for another scoop of cobbler. Doc, Charlie, Mom and Dad listened intrigued, as she explained more of what she had found in her research.

"The Mustangs gave the Indians a new way
of life for hunting and fighting."

Karilynn was pointing to things in her booklet and using her teacher's voice as she explained all these things.

"The Cherokee Indians were the best at breeding
the Mustangs and had large herds.

Mindy, show them your paintings," instructed Karilynn.

The three visitors at the table caught their breath in surprise. Mindy's paintings looked professional, and she handed Tomás the framed original of her painting of the horses as a gift.

Seven mustangs shared one canvas artistically arranged with each horse painted on a background of the territory where it traditionally roams. One ran through a field of high native grass. Others were painted with mountains, streams, and dry-land cactus as a background. Their colors ranged from the spotted blankets of the appaloosa, to a red dun, and a line back buckskin. There were two paint horses. But the most stunning one was the Splash Pinto painted with a large white area surrounded by a reddish-brown. Its face looked like it had been dipped into a bucket of white paint.

"Wow, you are a true artist," Tomás said, as he looked at his gift with wide-open eyes. "Not only a pretty good rider...but an artist as well," he said, searching for an English word...but gave up and just shrugged and smiled.

"Do mustang really come in all of these colors?" Josh asked

Clearing her voice, Karilynn, the teacher, brought her students back to the booklet. "These and more," Karilynn noted. "You can see from my research, that the original Spanish horse was the appaloosa. But with all the other breeds of horses that came along, almost every color can be found. Some mustangs are part Andalusia

I've named my booklet:

The Mustangs
Spirit of American Freedom
Symbol of the American West.

"Great title and great book, Karilynn!" Josh said with a mouth full of cobbler.

"Thanks, Josh," she said, not knowing whether he was teasing or not. "But now for the sad part. We had two million wild horses in 1900. Since then, many mustangs were hunted and sold for dog food."

"Today, they're under the Bureau of Land Management control, and the BLM feels that 27,000 horses are all that can be grazed on the 37 territories that are set aside for them. They want to do away with the extra horses. And even though many are adopted, at this point there are 33,000 roaming these 37 territories. And, yes the government wants to kill off the extras," Karilynn said with tears in her eyes. "Mustang advocates are fighting right now to keep that from happening."

"Oh," sighed Mindy. "And we are only going to bring back eight!"

"Yes," Dad said. "But that is eight more safe Mustangs that won't be turned into dog food."

"What color do you think you want?" asked Mom trying to change the sad mood.

"Oh, I know for sure," Mindy sounded off with excitement. "I want a paint, and Shannon wants an Appaloosa.

"As Doc has told us, we have to take what is available," Tomás said. "It is not like shopping at a Mall."

"That's right," Charlie said. "You get what you get and you don't pitch a fit."

Karilynn laughed, as that is what her teacher always said when they were passing out various cookies or candy.

"And no whining! Remember, grandpa does not like whining!" Charlie said with a wink.

***

Two mornings later Mom and Dad sat on the cabin porch drinking coffee. Dad had his feet propped on the porch railing and leaned back in the rocking chair, with a big smile on his face. Mom sat straight up in her rocker with a frown on her face.

"It's so quiet," Mom said with a worried voice.

"Yeah," Dad said with a peaceful sigh.

"No, I mean it's too quiet!! Do you think the children will be alright?" She sat up straighter, sniffing!

"Yes, I think definitely yes, they will be fine." Dan reached over and took her hand. "Do you hear the creek running, and the quiet wind in the pine trees?"

"I do, now that you mention it," Sherry said, with a surprised look on her face.

***

The morning that Shannon and Mindy left to go to Hi-Lonesome, they could hardly hold still, they were so excited.

Charlie, Mindy, Grandpa, and Tomás, rode in one pickup pulling six horses in a trailer. Shannon, her Dad and her 19 year old brother, Travis, pulled another trailer full of horses.

Two of grandpa's wranglers, Rip and Sam were in the third truck. Sam would cook and keep the campsite in order. Shannon's dad had brought along two wrangles from his ranch, Hal Dean and Joe.

When they had arrived at the campsite, Mindy was surprised by the accommodations. There were tent pads, a fire ring surrounded by rocks, and a corral for their horses. An outhouse was located behind a nearby tree. "The BLM have set these sites in places close to where the Mustangs roam," Charlie answered Mindy's unasked question. "Your grandpa had to sign us up for this campsite, and at that time fill out the paper work to capture eight mustangs."

The camp was in a clearing surrounded by deep green forest. "I love the smell of the forest," Shannon said to Mindy. Both girls sniffed and gave a big sigh.

Sam had parked his truck close to the campfire ring where he could cook from the back of the pickup using the big Coleman Camp Stove while the grilling was done at the wood fire. The wranglers and Charlie unloaded the horses and shouted for the kids to unload the tack. Sam set up tables under a tarp to keep the tack dry. The saddles were placed underneath the table. Ropes, harnesses, and saddle blankets, were put on top.

"It's early," Grandpa said. "Let's ride! It'll be good to give the horses some exercise and we can check out the lay of the land."

Grandpa did not have to ask twice. The girls and Tomás were saddled up and ready to go in ten minutes. When Grandpa and Charlie were ready, they set out. Grandpa motioned the kids up front and they started off in a gentle lope.

They followed a rough trail higher up in the mountains. After awhile, Charlie rode up beside them. They stopped. "Look down there!" Charlie pointed towards a cloud of dust. "Those are mustangs running! Follow me!"

Charlie led them down a steep hill. Tomás, Shannon, Mindy and Grandpa pulled up beside him. On this ridge, they could see a herd of nine mustangs stopped by a stream of water. A beautiful black stallion lifted his head, flatted his ears, and with a loud whinny started running his herd.

Even though they were above the horses, they could hear their hoofs pounding the ground. Mindy's heart was pounding in rhythm with their hoofs. Tomás felt like he was in one of the Old West movies that he had seen as a child, and he smiled at the tears he saw in the girl's eyes.

"I never get tired of seeing Mustangs run," Grandpa said. Even he and Charlie sat in awe of the beautiful horses.

"Did we spook them?" Mindy asked.

"No, look over there." Grandpa pointed to two wildcats sunning on a nearby rocky slope.

The mustangs had disappeared so the five riders returned to camp. Sam had a fire going and hotdogs and spuds on the grill over the campfire. The kids sat on logs around the fire.

"Hot dogs taste super cooked over the campfire," Shannon smiled, as she wiped mustard on her sleeve.

"I love American hotdogs," Tomás chimed in. With Oreos for dessert, they happily sat around and talked about Mustangs.

Later that night, Mindy and Shannon snuggled into their bedrolls in their tent. "I feel like I am in heaven," Mindy said with a yawn.

Tomás didn't drop off to sleep as quickly as the girls. He was just now realizing that catching a black stallion was going to be a lot harder than he had ever imagined, and wondered if he was really up for the task.

CHAPTER 16

RUNNING MUSTANGS

The next morning Sam packed a huge picnic lunch, and after breakfast the eight cowboys and two cowgirls started out on a search for their mustangs.

Sitting at the table last night, Grandpa and Charlie explained that they needed to roundup one herd with about eight mustangs.

"What if we don't find a herd with Shannon's appaloosa, and a Paint for me?" Mindy asked.

"The most important thing is for the herd to have a black stallion. That's what Tomás needs for his quest," Grandpa said gruffly. Joe rolled his eyes and smirked when Grandpa said that.

"That's right, I remember that we talked about that," Mindy said in a nice tone. Mindy did not know why, but all of a sudden she found that she wanted to please her Grandfather.

"What's up with that," she thought to herself. "I always thought of him as just a grumpy old man and now I want to please him?" Thinking it over, she could not come up with the answer.

Grandpa had a BLM map marked where the mustangs had last been seen. The group poured over it and decided who would ride out where.

Shannon's father, brother and the wranglers made up the first group. Grandpa, Charlie, Mindy, Tomás, and Shannon made up the second group.

Early the next morning when Grandpa said, "Let's ride!" ten eager riders set out to search for the mustangs.

Grandpa led their group up to the high meadows. They tied their horses to trees and walked a quarter of a mile to a ridge that over looked a creek that ran into a small lake. They counted three groups who came for water, but each herd had too few horses, and the only one with nine horses had a white stallion.

Mindy and Shannon watched in awe as the different herds watered. They counted off three duns and two palominos in the herd with the white stallion. After a short wait, the third herd came up to water and had a black stallion. His females were three dark bays. There was a Gullo mare. She was slate grey with black spots and a black mane and tail. "She's beautiful! I could live with her if I don't get my paint," Mindy whispered. The men took note of the small herd with that black stallion.

Mindy saw out of the corner of her eye Grandpa's surprised look that they could name the different coat colors in the herd. That made her smile inside.

They ate lunch and waited about an hour before another herd roamed toward the water. "Look at that black stallion," Tomás whispered excitedly.

"And nine in the herd!" Mindy said to Grandpa.

"Looks good," Grandpa answered back with a small smile.

Just a few minutes later, Charlie pointed toward a cloud of dust heading toward the watering hole. The black stallion raised his head and flattened his ears. His whole body stiffened up, shaking with fury. When the small herd came into view, he went out to meet the white stallion.

"That stallion wants some of Blackie's mares," Charlie said out loud. He figured that they did not need to be so quiet right now. "Get ready for a fight."

The two stallions approached each other slowly. Their eyes were wide open and huge. They spread their feet and with heads down, flared their nostrils and shook their heads, snorting at each other. Then the fight began. Both horses reared up and came down bucking and kicking. They lunged out to bite. The men watched in amazement, but both Shannon and Mindy were shaking in their boots.

The black stallion fought fearlessly, kicking, biting, and rearing up to land hard on the white's head. It was a fierce, bloody fight. Finally the white stallion limped away covered with blood. His herd followed slowly behind him.

Mindy looked at Shannon's scared face. Shannon was struggling to keep back tears. To Mindy it had seemed frightful and sad. But Tomás stood silently, his face showing no reaction.

"Boy, those stallions really know how to mix it up," Charlie laughed.

"They do battle fiercely to keep their herds," Grandpa answered back. "Not very many folks have seen that in real life," he said turning towards the kids. "It's part of nature's way," he explained when he saw the girl's faces.

"Yes it is," Mindy agreed, but her voice sounded strained even to her own ears. She was glad when he turned away. Maybe he hadn't seen how the fight had effected them. She did not want her Grandpa to think they were too big of sissies to be involved in the roundup.

"I'm hungry," Charlie said. "Fighting always gives me an appetite…Well, I wasn't fighting, but you know what I mean."

"I don't know what you mean," said Tomás, "but I sure am hungry."

The girls were glad to have something else to think about. They somberly said, "Yep, you always are."

He shrugged and went to retrieve the saddlebags with their lunch. Out came bread and butter sandwiches, cold fried chicken, pickles, chips, beer and cokes. For desert, they found oranges and Aunt Netta's peanut butter cookies and brownies.

"Sam is my kind of cook," Shannon said contentedly.

When they were "plum filled up" as Charlie said, they spent the next couple of hours taking it easy. Charlie and Grandpa snoozed with their heads' on their saddles. In the heat of the day the mustangs would not return to the water hole. Tomás wrote in his journal, while Shannon had brought a book to read. Mindy pulled out her sketchpad to draw the mountain lake and surrounding beauty.

About three o'clock, two new herds showed up to water, but they were too small. When five o'clock rolled around they decided to head back to camp.

At dinner they discussed what each group had spotted.

"We saw five herds," Rip said, "but only one with a black stallion leader."

"I don't think that Tomás would think that stallion was good enough for his choice," Joe said sarcastically. Then he laughed to cover the sneer in his voice. No one seemed to notice his tone, but Tomás did.

"Your right," Shannon's brother said. "He was small, and had a big scar across his wither. Small horse, big fighter," he chuckled.

The discussion returned to the black stallion and mares that Grandpa's group had found. There were two other spots in this immediate area where mustangs had been sighted and the discussion centered on whether to check them out.

"What other coat colors were in his herd?" Shannon's dad asked.

Shannon and Mindy looked at each other and then at the rest of their team. "We all got so involved with the fight that we were just looking at the stallions," Charlie said.

Tomás spoke up, "I remember one black appaloosa, and thinking how happy Shannon would be with that mare."

Mindy added, "I remember a Gullo and a beautiful paint. Shannon said she remembered the appaloosa and a lineback dun.

The men decided that the group would start out early the next morning to find that herd. If the stallion and the mares still struck their fancy, they would look no further.

Later that night Tomás, Mindy, and Shannon sat together in the girls' tent. "That fight was horrible. I wonder if the white stallion survived?" Mindy asked thoughtfully.

"I talked to my Dad about it. He says that he can read my face and it told him I was upset!" Shannon replied. "We talked awhile. He explained that most stallions will fight, then move on and recover."

"I just had no idea that horses could fight like that. The bellowing, the sound of their hoofs striking…It was awful!" Mindy teared up.

Tomás was strangely quiet.

"Didn't it bother you?" Shannon asked.

"No," he responded. Mindy looked for his smiling eyes. They were not smiling but had turned cold.

"What?" she asked. "You're upset too. I can see it in your eyes. What's wrong?" she questioned him.

"The horse fight did not bother me because I have seen members of my own family covered in blood and even shot dead." He swallowed back a sob. "I should not have said that." Tomás got up and rushed out of the tent.

Mindy and Shannon just sat there looking at each other. They hardly knew what to think, much less say!

A little later, Charlie stuck his head in their tent. Sitting down, he looked at the girls' sad faces. Tomás has seen some very bad things in his life. In Spanish he told me, "El siento dolor… he feels pain that he spoke about that part of his life. He didn't want you to know."

"When he told me about some of the hard stuff in his life, it led him to telling me that he feels in danger right now. I asked him to tell you about it, saying you two could handle it. That we would help and figure things out together." Charlie thought a minute, and then said, "It might be very bad business. Can you handle it?"

"I think so," Shannon answered slowly.

"I hope so," Mindy said.

"Ok, then. Let him come talk to you. I think he will."

The next morning Mindy sat down at breakfast next to Tomás. She didn't say a word, but reached over and squeezed his hand when she got up. They rode all day, but could not find the herd. Several other herds were sighted, but none seemed right. They got up the next morning to ride out again. Grandpa and Charlie had decided to divide and conquer. Two groups would ride in two different directions from the mountain lake where they had seen what they were now calling their black mustang herd.

"Let's change groups," Joe suggested cunningly. "I would like to ride with Mr. Charlie and Mr. Cunningham. I have much to learn about mustangs. Besides, a change might bring us good luck," he said.

"Well, I don't believe in luck," Grandpa growled. "We are teamed up this way for a purpose, so we stay the same. See you here at camp at three thirty. Let's ride!"

Joe pulled off his hat, waved it in the air, and shouted, "Lets go!" He loped off with his group.

When Mindy's and Grandpa's group returned to camp, Rip and his men were sitting there with big smiles on their faces. "We found them about an hour ago. I left Joe there to keep an eye on them. He will ride in later and let us know where they bedded down for the night."

"Good," Grandpa said. "We'll ride out early in the morning." The rest of the day was spent getting the supplies organized for the trip back to Hi-Lonesome.

Later, grandpa sat them all down and pulled out his maps to show everyone their trail back to the ranch. "With any luck, we should be able to drive the herd back in eight days. Here we are," grandpa said, pointing to Grand Junction on the map. "Here and here it's straight shooting. We'll ride down to Mesa National Park and over night there where the grazing is good. Here we cross the Gunnison River, where the snow melt hopefully has not yet swelled it to the spring flooding stage."

"Now here's the hardest part…two different times we'll cross over the Continental Divide…here on our way to Crested Butte, where we'll spend the night, and here where we go over Tin Cup Pass." Grandpa pointed to both spots on the map. "It's a steep ride over the Divide because it tops out around 11,300 feet. At that elevation, humans are breathless and the horses are sweating and breathing hard. We'll cross it again here at Tin Cup Pass where we'll spend the night in town. And then, in the blink of an eye, we'll be back at Hi-Lonesome."

Dinner that evening was Sam's giant double cheeseburgers and barbeque beans cooked over the fire. They all had smiling faces until Joe rode in. "I lost them," Joe said. "I know you'll blame me," he grumped. "That stallion is tricky." He sat down, head bowed sadly, yet Mindy noticed a sly look on his face.

Everyone sat quietly waiting to hear what Grandpa would say. "I still say we go tomorrow," Charlie spoke up.

"You think so?" Grandpa asked.

"We'll find em again. That's what my gut says, anyhow," Charlie said.

"And I'm supposed to trust your gut?" Grandpa asked. Charlie nodded his head. "Ok then," Grandpa said. "We ride out at first light."

CHAPTER 17

THE BIG POW-WOW

After dessert, Thomas asked Mindy if he could talk to her privately.

They walked away from the campsite and sat down on a log.

"Lo siento," Tomás said in a quiet voice.

"English, please," Mindy said squeezing his hand softly.

"Oh yes!" Tomás said slowly. Mindy could tell that he was translating from Spanish to English in his mind. "I am sorry that I told you about seeing people killed. I did not want you to know about that part of my life. Being the prince of a country...well, there are a lot of wonderful things about it. But hard times come with it also. In my country, the danger is with the drugs cartels."

"But now, it is better. We have forced the cartels out. My family is strong...with a small but loyal army. We rule fairly and with justice. Our people are safe. They do not fear the government or the army as people do in other countries. But the cartels are always looking for a way back in."

Tomás went on talking about seeing his grandfather murdered. He had even seen his mother get shot. She was not killed, but wounded. Mindy listened in stunned silence as he told her the frightful things that Tomás and his family had faced.

"You know me, Mindy. There is much good in my life, too," Tomás said, his face brightening.

"Yes, she answered. "I would never have known that you had faced such dangers. I should have, though. Last year, at the end of the summer, some uniformed men rode up to our fort. You know, the one I showed you on the creek? They explained that they were securing the area so it would be safe for the prince."

"That threw us for a loop and we never figured it out. Looking back, I can see now, it had to be for you," Mindy said with a smile.

At one point we thought the prince might be a bully at school whose last name is Prinz. He gave all of us a rough time. And we have to ride the school bus with him every day."

"What does this word bully mean?" queried Tomás.

Mindy explained. "You know, a mean kid who picks on others and threatens them." Tomás had understood her, but she could see he was chewing on something else in his mind.

"I am not surprised that you saw the men looking around," Thomas said with a scowl. "They probably went riding around the whole ranch, talked to your grandfather, and checked out the neighboring towns.

My father believes I am still a child, while I want to be on my own without guardianes following me around."

"I thought I would be safe here! I felt safe with your grandfather, Charlie and your aunt. But now I am not so sure," he frowned.

"What do you mean?" Mindy asked wide-eyed.

"Joe…I am almost sure he was sent here to harm me, or perhaps even kidnap me. Have you seen the way he watches me all the time and says strange things like, 'We won't find a mustang here good enough for Tomás.' Then he laughs like he does not mean anything by it. When I first talked to Charlie, he said I was imagining it. But after watching Joe and thinking about the things I told him, he now agrees with me."

An image of Joe's bowed head with a cunning look on his face at dinner flashed into Mindy's mind. "We need a pow-wow with Charlie," Mindy said. "Can I tell Shannon about what's going on?"

"Yes, I think that is a good idea. I could not explain all of this to her. It is so painful to me that I wanted it to be just you, my closest friend."

"I get it," Mindy said solemnly. "I am glad to be your closest friend," she said with a shy smile. "I do trust Shannon, though, and will explain some of it to her…maybe not everything. Ok?"

"Ok", he said sadly. "A pow-wow. If that means a meeting then, yes, we must have a pow-wow."

"All right then, tonight before bed. Everyone will think we are just talking like we usually do before we turn in." Plans made, they returned to the campfire.

After dinner, they all chatted around the campfire as usual. Mindy and Shannon tried to laugh and talk with the others and act like it was any other night.

Right before they returned to their tents, Charlie and the kids met, sat down, and pow-wowed. Mindy had already talked to Shannon, explaining some of the things about Tomás' life. Actually, it was the first time that Shannon knew about Tomás being a prince.

Charlie explained everything he and Tomás had noticed about Joe. Mindy listened closely, but Shannon sat there with a dazed look on her face. "That's why I thought we should ride out tomorrow," Charlie said. "I bet Joe chased those horses away. Rip can take us to where he last saw them and we can track them from there. I know they didn't go far. This is their territory!"

They decided on a plan to protect Tomás from Joe. "It is not a sure fire thing, but it's a pretty good plan," Charlie said nodding his head. "Two rough old birds, and you kids…well, I think we are up for this fight."

Grandpa had been told about the danger to Tomás and was furious about the threats. Tomás seemed out of sorts. As they headed off to their tents, Tomás mumbled under his breath, "Here I am, being baby sat again."

"Bet we won't get much sleep tonight," Mindy whispered to Shannon as they lowered the flap on their tent.

***

Early the next morning, they saddled up and rode out. Charlie's hunch proved correct and after an hour they had found the mustangs again. Ten riders made a quick job of rounding up the herd. Now they were headed for Mesa National Park.

Hooves pounding, dust flying, the mustangs ran full out for over an hour. Bandanas covered the riders' noses to keep out the dust, but Mindy could see Tomás' eyes as he rode beside her. They glistened, and she knew that he had a smile on his face.

When they had mounted up that morning, Tomás had said to her, "Mindy, you know, I feel like John Wayne. I read where he once said…'Courage is being scared to death, but saddling up anyway.' I hope I can ride like him and fight like him if I have to!" They both had felt light hearted as they climbed into their saddles. Mindy was chuckling to herself that he not only knew the famous cowboy star, but could quote one of his well-known sayings.

All day the horses kept up a quick pace. In early afternoon they herded the horses into a large corral at Mesa National Park with a campsite nearby. A small stream ran through the corral and Mindy and Shannon laughed as they sat on the fence and listened to the horses slurping water.

The stallion paced and stomped, fighting being enclosed in the corral. Later the wranglers herded the mares out of the corral to graze. They would not leave their stallion far behind, and grazed peacefully on the nearby grass. Tomás fed the stallion grain from their supplies. However, he didn't want food. He wanted out of the corral with his mares running freely with him.

It took everyone working together to keep him away from the gate as they herded the mares back into the corral. With his family returned, the stallion settled down.

As darkness fell, the night lit up with a million starts. There were no city lights to dull the brightness of the night sky. The kids laid down gazing up at the sky and talking quietly. One by one they drifted off into a deep sleep. Rip and Hal Dean traded watches to guard the herd through the night. Everyone else slept hard after their long ride. Daylight found them on the trail again.

The mustangs set a fast pace all morning. Near noon, Grandpa had the herd rounded up to rest and drink at a small lake. "Rip, you and Joe start out at a slower pace. We'll heard them in behind you and keep them moving slower. These mustangs have lived on the open range so they have more endurance than our ranch horses."

Mindy was glad for the slower pace. Her body hurt from head to toe, but now she was able to relax in her saddle. They rode through a beautiful green valley with forest on either side. The sky was deep Colorado blue, and the air was fresh and clean.

They stopped about supper time. Joe, Charlie and Hal Dean had ridden ahead to set up a collapsible corral. Tomás sat on his horse looking at the strange contraption.

"We don't have those in my country," Tomás said to the girls.

"Yep, it is quite a contraption," Shannon said.

"I thought it was called a corral," Tomás said, with confusion in his eyes. Mindy and Shannon laughed. Tomás laughed, too, but he was not quite sure what was so funny.

The next two days passed exactly like the first two. "A routine," Charlie said. "A routine is a good thing for greenhorns like you." His smile widened as the kids frowned.

"*Routine*," Mindy said with her hands on her hips. "Routine is washing dinner dishes, going to school every day, and doing homework. That's routine. *Not* herding mustangs…no way. This is an adventure! And I am not a greenhorn."

Charlie, Tomás, and Shannon laughed out loud when Mindy stomped off.

On day five, they noticed that the trail was beginning to get steeper. The air was thinner and colder, but the Mustangs didn't seem to notice. They kept the usual pace, and would have broken into a run if the cowboys had not kept the pace under control.

At the end of the day the trees had disappeared and only the stunted growth of small bushes and gnarled trees could be seen. There were big patches of snow everywhere and a new coldness in the air.

Early wild flowers pushed out of the frozen ground and peeked through the snow adding a show of color to the high mountain ridge.

"It looks like a fairy land," Mindy said with a sigh, as they sat near the small mountain lake close to where they were camped. "But where are the trees?"

"We're above tree line now," Shannon explained. "Trees cannot live up this high. I think Grandpa said that we're above 11,000 feet. That's why it's so cold and why it's hard for us to breathe…thin air. Just like your Grandpa warned us."

"Want to race to the campfire?" Tomás asked.

"No way!" both girls said at the same time.

The campfire was set up in an old fire ring behind huge rocks that broke the cold wind.

Later, sitting around the fire, Charlie told them that they were sitting on the top of the Continental Divide.

"We read about it in geography, but I didn't know you could sit on it in Colorado," Shannon laughed.

"Yep," Charlie laughed with her. "When we herd the horses over Tin Cup Pass, you'll be able to see the first railroad tunnel that went through the Divide."

Grandpa and Tomás took the night watch to keep an eye on the stallion and his mares. But at first light they were up and moving along with everyone else. The riders started down the mountain, a slow and steep descent sometimes covered with snow. Even the mustangs were poking along on this side of the divide.

Suddenly, there was a high pitched whiney from a horse near the back of the group. Tomás, Shannon, and Mindy turned and saw a mustang go down and slide into a big rock. Charlie rushed passed and yelled to Grandpa, "Keep them moving. I'll tend to this and catch up."

Mindy gasped when she saw the horse was "her" black and white paint. She leaned out of her saddle to whisper to Shannon. "Stay close to Tomás until we get back." In the confusion Mindy thought Joe might take the opportunity to do something to Tomás. Shannon nodded her head as the herd moved on down the steep trail.

Mindy rode up to Charlie and slipped off of her horse. Kneeling down beside him, one look at his face showed her the seriousness of the injury. Charlie shook his head and stood up. Mindy slid up to the horse's head. The horse was snorting and trembling. She rubbed her head and muzzle. "Leave, Mindy," Charlie said in a stern voice.

"No," she answered. "I know what you have to do, and I'm staying."

"I hate to do this," Charlie groaned. "Two legs are broken. I want you to go. I can't put her down with you here watching."

"I'm not going," Mindy answered. She kept her hand on the mare's head. Charlie pulled out his gun, and with one shot it was over. Mindy stayed until the horse stop breathing. She silently got up and mounted her horse.

Charlie laid his hand on her saddle. "She's out of her misery now, Mindy." He saw the tears streaming down her face as she nodded. "Let's ride, little darling," Charlie said quietly.

It took them twenty minutes to catch up with the herd. Tomás pulled up beside her, reached for her hand and squeezed it hard. She nodded to him, using her sleeve to dry her face.

Late in the afternoon the trail flattened out and they drove the horses into a corral right outside of Crested Butte. The Butte was a small, old mountain town, that skiing and tourism had kept on the map. It was surrounded by tall mountain peaks, some still wearing their winter snow. The town itself, leveled out into wide, green valleys.

"We aren't too far from home," Grandpa said. "But our horses need a break. We'll leave late in the morning." Hal Dean and Rip volunteered to stay with the herd, while the others went into town for their first real food in six days.

"Steak," Charlie said with a hungry look in his eyes.

"You got that right," Grandpa agreed. He asked at the General Store where to find the best steaks in town. They found the Hungry Rustler on the main street and sat down to steaks, baked potatoes and home style green beans.

"I'm stuffed," said Mindy, after sharing a steak with Shannon. "But I saw ice cream next to the souvenir shop. We can't let that pass by," she said, her eyes sparkling, "can we?"

"I think I can squeeze in one scoop," Shannon laughed.

"No problem for me to eat a big bowl of ice cream," Tomás chuckled.

To their surprise, Grandpa included a night in a small hotel except for those guarding the herd. Charlie had gone back to keep an eye on the horses while Rip and Hal Dean ate supper. "Thanks, but no hotel for me," Rip said. "Me and Hal Dean would rather be under the stars."

Shannon and Mindy looked forward to sleeping in late since they would not start the drive until 11am. The next morning, Mindy whispered, "Are you awake, Shannon?"

"Yeah, I am now." she sighed.

"I thought I heard you rolling around over there. What time is it?" Mindy questioned.

"The clock says 7:00, but it must be later. We said we were going to sleep in."

"Well, at least the sun is up," Mindy stretched and yawned, "and I feel like I slept on a feather bed!!! I'd forgotten how good a real mattress feels," Mindy yawned again.

"Let's go wake Tomás up," Shannon suggested with a laugh.

Downstairs, in the hotel cafe Charlie told them that Tomás was still asleep. Mindy grabbed a glass of water and she and Shannon headed up the stairs. With Charlie's key, they quietly opened the door. As it creaked open, Tomás mumbled in his sleep and turned over on his side. Tiptoeing to the bed they giggled quietly as Tomás slept. Mindy poured the cold water on top of his head. Surprisingly, Tomás flew out of bed slinging snow all over the girls.

"I knew you were coming," he laughed, "but I did not know you were going to get me with cold water. I hoped to surprise you with snow. I was out at six o'clock this morning scooping up snow in those shady places close to the corral."

"Yuck, Tomás!" Shannon said with a giggle as she eyed the brown snow. Let's go change clothes, Mindy.

"Good idea," Mindy said, "but we'll be back. So you had better watch out, Tomás."

CHAPTER 18

TIN CUP BURGERS

Shannon and Mindy caught up with Tomás at the corral. The ranch hands were talking about the trails they wanted to cover that day. Tomás watched them with leery eyes as the girls walked up to him. "Peace!" Shannon said and stuck out her hand. Tomás quickly grabbed her hand with a look of relief.

"At least for now," Mindy said with a wicked grin. "Tomorrow is another day. Grandpa said we could hang out in town until it's time to go."

They visited the old fashion school, looked at the black smith shop, and bought souvenirs. The girls bought Tomás a hand carved black stallion painted with Indian symbols. He bought a picture frame with Colorado carved at the bottom. "Now all I need is a picture of the three of us for this souvenir," he said.

The girls bought colorful cowboy bandanas covered with horses and two sterling and turquoise charms on matching necklaces.

They returned to camp to find a safe place for their important purchases. As Mindy was tucking her souvenirs into her saddlebags, she gave a small gasp. She spotted BF Bear's head peeking out. "Whoa," he growled softly. "Trouble on the way." He put a paw to his mouth to signal her to say no more.

They saddled up, ready to go. A few minutes later the others joined them and they set off for the small town of Tin Cup, home of Charlie's favorite hamburgers.

Charlie had talked to the kids the night before about Tomás and his family's troubles. "Well, safe so far," Charlie had said. "But 'til we get Tomás back to the ranch, we gotta be on the lookout for danger."

"But perhaps Joe plans to kidnap him from the ranch where people won't notice he's missing as quickly," Mindy said. She knew trouble was brewing. The Bear always knows!

"Or maybe Joe has some accomplices coming to help him kidnap Tomás on our trip back," Charlie said with unease. "But we've got a good plan, so we've got your back, Tomás. And we'll all keep our eyes wide open." Tomás said nothing as he drew in a deep breath and nodded.

They left Crested Butte and immediately started up into the high mountains where they would crest the Continental Divide for the second time. Mindy could not get rid of the feeling that eyes were watching them from the forest. Had the drug lord's men already joined up with Joe to kidnap Tomás? However, she corralled her fears while riding the narrow trail. The altitude and snow forced them to ride at a slower pace. Even so, the short distance to Tin Cup found them herding the horses into a corral after a three hour ride.

Tin Cup was a smaller mountain town and it had fewer visitors than Crested Butte. It was harder to reach, with very few places to stay. Eight old wooden buildings lined a rough dirt road that stretched the length of greater downtown Tin Cup.

Gold had been the catalyst for the settlement back in the late 1800's. The rough living miners brought with them their frequent fights, free flowing whiskey, and deadly shootouts.

To the southwest of town, four small knolls made up the town's cemetery. Catholics, Jews, and Protestants were buried separately on their own small hill. The last knoll, Boot Hill, was full of unmarked graves of rough characters. Unless a visitor had read the history of the town, someone passing through would not have guessed the violent past of Tin Cup.

Nowadays, Tin Cup was a small peaceful town, surrounded by small lakes and streams, and the bright blue Colorado Sky.

"Right there is the best hamburger in the US of A," Charlie said, as he pointed to a shack on a small lake. "Let's eat!" This time Joe and Hal Dean stayed with the horses at the corral with a promise of burgers to come. The rest of the group followed the smell of greasy, old fashioned hamburgers and settled around a table in the restaurant. Tomás went out back to the men's room just in time to see Joe headed back toward the corral.

"*Que paso, Jose,*" Tomás called after him. Joe turned around without hesitation to answer his Spanish name. When he realized what he had done, he walked over to Tomás.

"*Ya sabes?*" he snarled at Tomás. You know?

"*Si, ya lo se.*" Tomás answered back in a calm voice. "I know who you are." They continued speaking in Spanish.

Joe angrily replied, "I'm here to keep an eye on you and keep my employer up to date. The deaths in your own family have proved that Emilio Sanchez does not take no for an answer to his business propositions." Joe stormed off glaring back over his shoulder.

Tomás's heart jumped into his throat at Jose's threats. He stopped outside the small restaurant, took a deep breath and wondered what John Wayne would do now. Plastering a weak smile on his face, he reentered and sat down biting into a large cheese burger.

"Best burger ever," Tomás said, while wiping the mustard off his face and praying his fear wasn't showing.

"Exactly how many hamburgers have you had since you came here?" Rip asked.

"Quite a few. I hang out with the two burger queens and Charlie…and they know good burgers. If Charlie says it is the best, then I believe him!"

"Fair enough," Rip laughed.

After lunch they decided to visit the nearby grave yard. "Let me get Charlie. I heard him say he wanted to see his great, great uncle's grave," Tomás said.

They wandered around Boot Hill, first looking at the few headstones they could find. "There sure are a lot of unmarked graves," Mindy said.

"Yep," Charlie mused. "Rough characters came in during the gold rush with ideas about getting rich quick off of someone else's sweat and hard work. Sometimes they found ways to steal a claim or another minor's gold. But these minors were tough old birds. They fought for their claims and accounted for a lot of these unmarked graves."

"Look at that grave over there and what's written on the headstone," Charlie pointed.

Bob Rivers
Shot the Sheriff, Charles Waters, July 2, 1890
Killed by Tin Cup Residents, July 3, 1890
Mama told Bob to live by The Good Book
But he didn't listen. He lived by gun.

"Yep, the sheriff that he killed was my great, great uncle. Bob River's sister came up a year later with the stone and marked his grave."

"Is your Uncle buried here?" Tomás asked.

"Yep. Over on the Protestant hill." The group wandered through the graveyard amazed at the old dates. Some of the dates revealed a child born and died on the same day. Or others, whose birth and death dates were only a few years apart.

"This one says Charles Waters," Shannon said.

"Yep, that is my great Uncle Charlie. Hear tell that he was an honest sheriff who worked hard to keep the peace. Tin Cup was a safer place for the three years he was in office."

His stone read.

CHARLIE RIVERS
Good man
Good Sherriff
Good enough for God
Died July 2, 1890

"OK, that's enough for me," Charlie said. The kids all followed him back across the bridge into town.

After a warm breakfast at the restaurant the next morning, the group saddled up for the last day of the great Mustang Round Up. Mindy and Shannon would have been sad that it was ending, but they were too worried about keeping Tomás safe. Mindy looked around and could see her friends riding tall in their saddles. No slouching today. They were all on high alert after Charlie's latest pow-wow with the wranglers (minus Joe, of course) and kids about the conversation outside of the burger joint.

She and Tomás rode side by side. Charlie followed close behind. Grandpa was on the far side and Rip rode in front of him. Shannon rode up front with her Dad.

They kept the horses at a slow and steady pace. As they rode by Mirror Lake, strong winds rose up making the June day feel chilly. Finally, they started down the last steep stretch towards the Hi-Lonesome Ranch.

About five miles out from the ranch, Mindy felt as if the watching eyes had returned yet again. Her unsettled stomach grew worse and her heart began to beat faster. They passed to the south of St. Elmo, a ghost town that shared the same valley as the ranch. The landscape leveled out. The open trail was edged with a wide creek and forests.

Suddenly, six men on horseback sprang out of the forest and raced toward them. Even more amazing were the two moose that broke from the trees opposite the riders and crossed the creek to join the fight.

Mindy realized that she had been right. The eyes of Tomás's enemies had been watching them. But the eyes of their friends were watching, too. Mindy rode on the alert waiting for the signal to execute her part of the plan that Grandpa and Charlie had laid out for Tomás' escape.

Before the bad guys could pull their guns, Grandpa raised up his rifle and shot into the air. The startled mustangs stampeded with Rip and Hal Dean hot on their trail. Tomás and Mindy were ready for the shot and charged along side of the stampeding mustangs, putting the horses between them and danger.

Senor Sanchez's riders were surprised to see grandpa's men stop and turn towards them with guns drawn. That sent then them racing back to the safety of the trees.

However, Joe had not been tricked by the gunshot. He raced toward the running mustangs hoping he was right about Tomás' escape route. He pulled out his gun and aimed at Rip and Hal Dean. But before he could fire, a moose lumbered up and knocked him from his horse. Joe jumped up reaching for his saddle but the big moose knocked him back to the ground. With feet firmly planted on his chest, she said, "It is not mannerly, *not at all,* to harm a prince or his friends."

Joe lay on the ground afraid to move. One thought floated through his mind. "I must have bonked my head. I thought that moose talked to me." Then he blacked out from the fall.

Mindy and Tomás cut away from the herd that continued to race down the trail. They rushed into the covering of the forest, and pushed on through the trees for about fifteen minutes. Mindy held up her hand signaling Tomás to a stop.

"Turquoise Lake is just over that point. It will be a rugged trip up, but we can safely spend the night there," Mindy said, breathing hard from the fast ride.

"Can they find us there?" Tomás asked.

"I don't think they will. It's so far off the beaten trail. But just to be sure, we won't camp too close to the lake."

Mindy started up toward the ridge. Finally, they had to dismount and lead the horses up and over slick rocks before they reached the top. Tomás looked down on a small mountain lake. It sparkled blue, so clear that the snow covered mountains behind it reflected like a photo in the lake.

"It's a glacier lake," Mindy explained. That's why it is such a spectacular color. After catching their breath, Mindy led Tomás down to the lake. The tired horses waded in and slurped up a good drink. When they had finished drinking, Tomás followed Mindy deep into the forest to camp for the night.

After unsaddling the horse and securing them to trees where they could munch on the fresh mountain grass, they found a old log to sit down on. They sat tiredly for a long time catching their breath. Mindy's heart was still racing and she wondered if Tomás' heart felt like hers." She reached over and put her hand over his heart.

She laughed out loud. "I thought I was the only one whose heart was pounding. Yours is, too, I see."

"I cannot smile," Tomás said sadly. "I have put you and your family and friends in grave danger."

Mindy did not mind the danger as long as they were able to keep Tomás safe. But she knew that it would do no good to say so at that moment.

"I am afraid for you as well as for the rest of us," Mindy said.

Tomás just looked at the ground with his sad eyes. They shared some of the food that they had packed. Mindy only ate a little as she knew she would soon be leaving Tomás behind. He would need all the extra food for the time they planned on hiding him under the water fall.

They unrolled their bedrolls with the plan that Mindy would take the first watch. As soon as he lay down, Tomás fell fast asleep. Mindy found BF Bear in her bedroll, and saw moose eyes peering out from the forest. No human needed to keep watch this night. She closed her eyes and dropped into a deep sleep.

In the early morning, Mindy felt a push on her back. She opened her eyes and looked up into a long-snouted face. The stars were fading from the sky, and the morning light would be coming soon.

The bear snuffled and stretched. "Whoa, its time to go," he said to Mindy. "Early birds get worm and all that," he quoted. "We don't want to be anybody's worm," he chuckled at his small joke. Mindy got the point. They needed to be on the trail before Tomás' kidnappers started searching for them again.

She woke Tomás who was more than ready to get an early start.

They decided to eat on the move. As Mindy picked up her saddle bags, she noticed one seemed very heavy. She looked inside and laughed.

"Look at this Tomás. Food!" She pulled out 12 biscuits, a chunk of cheese, and slices of cooked ham and beef. Six candy bars where hiding at the bottom of the saddle bag. "Somebody doesn't want you to starve."

"But how did it get here?" Tomás asked. Mindy heard a moose brumble quietly in the woods.

"Don't look at me," Mindy snickered. She would have to thank Manners Moose later. She filled two biscuits with ham. Then they saddled up and rode down to the lake. While the horses were drinking water, they enjoyed the mystery food. Both munched quietly, saying nothing.

Mindy reached over from her saddle to squeeze Tomás' hand, giving him a big smile. He smiled back, then prodded his horse to move out. Both knew the next step in the plan for Tomás' safety.

"I wish this adventure was over," Mindy thought. She was afraid for Tomás as well as for herself.

An hour's ride brought them to the part of Chalk Creek that ran into the stream by the secret waterfall. They sat quietly for a minute and just looked at each other. Then Tomás slid off his horse and handed Mindy his reigns. She watched Tomás walk off with only his bedroll and a heavy bag of food. With tears streaming down her face, she rode off, leading his horse toward the ranch.

CHAPTER 19

MINDY FACES DANGER

For the next hour, Mindy rode towards the ranch keeping to the deep woods. Her heart was thudding again. She did not want to say so, not even to herself. But she was afraid, very afraid. What would she do if Sanchez's men spotted her? What would she do if they caught her?

"Whoooah. Don't forget me!" said a voice that seemed to know what she was thinking.

"I won't forget you, courageous friend. It's a relief to have you along," Mindy answered with a small sob.

She would be passing the old Creek Mine before she could get to the ranch. There was no way around it unless she rode out into the open country where she would be an easy target for someone on the lookout.

"But the mine would be a great place for their hideout. What if that's where they've been camping?"

"Courage," whooahed BF Bear.

"Ok, BF, I'm gonna ride by the mine. That open space is just too dangerous." Mindy tugged on Trail Blazer's reigns as she rode off towards the mine.

Closer to the mine, she slipped off Lady. Leaving both horses behind, she crept up to the mine. To her relief it was empty. No fire rings, no horses, no signs of life at all. Just an old worn out building with rusting mining equipment. She ran back to the horses, mounted up and was on her way.

She chose a small deer trail and followed it up and over the mine.

Fifteen minutes later she was looking down at the house and barns of Hi-Lonesome. She wound her way down the hill to the ranch and wearily slid off her horse. Charlie ran out from the barn and grabbed her into a big bear hug.

"Girl, you're a sight for sore eyes!" Charlie exclaimed. "I've been watching for you all morning."

Charlie's warm hug and the sense of finally being safe were too much for Mindy. She burst into tears and wailed! He gave her another bear hug and patted her back. "You're safe now," he whispered.

Charlie spotted Grandpa and Aunt Netta over Mindy's shoulder. They, too, had been anxiously waiting and rushed out onto the porch when they heard the horses ride in. Aunt Netta wanted to run out and grab Mindy up, but Grandpa laid a gentle hand on her shoulder to hold her back. When Mindy's tears ran out and only quiet sniffles were left, they also went to hug Mindy.

"Glad to see you safe," Grandpa mumbled.

Mindy wiped her nose on the sleeve of her shirt. She didn't want Grandpa to think she was a cry baby. "Thanks," she said wiping her nose again.

Aunt Netta hugged and hugged her. "I'm so glad you're safe," she said in the middle of her own tears.

"Now, we need to get Tomás back safe," Mindy said, as a big tear slid down her face. "Oh dear," she thought. "I can't start bawling again."

Charlie saw her working hard to hold back her tears. He rescued her by speaking words of encouragement. "Let's go to the house and talk. Remember, we have a plan in place to rescue Tomás. We'll go and get him as soon as it's safe."

Aunt Netta took Mindy's hand and started back to the house. "I have biscuits and gravy saved for you." She stopped short with a worried look on her face. "I hope Tomás doesn't get too hungry in his hiding place. That boy eats more food than any teenager I've ever seen."

A small smile crept across Mindy's face. "I think he'll survive," she said, remembering the saddle bag of food from the Moose delivery service.

Getting Tomás home was easier than they thought. Charlie and Grandpa rounded up Joe and safely delivered him to the sheriff. When the FBI arrived to interrogate Joe, they explained the consequences of his involvement in the international drug trade. Joe had easily cracked and spilled the beans. The rest of Senor Sanchez's gang had been captured that night at their campsite. Fortunately for Mindy, they had camped out at the Lucky Strike mine on the far side of the ranch.

Charlie and Mindy had arrived early the next morning at the waterfall and found Tomás anxiously waiting to get back to the ranch. His sad face had lit up like the sun when he heard the gang had been captured. No more danger to his friends or to himself.

Shannon was waiting at the ranch when they rode up with Tomás. She threw her arms around both of her friends with a sigh of relief.

***

June turned into July and all the Cunninghams were back at the cabin.

Josh strutted around for days like he was an NFL stud. Karilynn had won awards for her outstanding new fire fighting techniques. Every night at dinner she told funny stories about her new friends and shared deep thoughts about what she had learned.

Mindy shared about her adventures with the Mustangs. Her brother and sister sat on the edge of their seats with wide eyes, listening to every detail. Dad looked at Mindy with pride in his eyes. Doc and Killer were invited over every night to share in all of the kids' summer adventures. Mom still fretted over the many dangers Mindy had faced. From morning to evening she was found in the kitchen cooking yet another meal or making a new dessert.

Mom would often mumble under her breath, still angry at Grandpa and her husband for the many dangerous situations they had let Mindy get into. Several times Mindy found her dad sitting on the couch listening to mom as she fussed and shook her finger at him.

Mindy would then pop into the room and interrupt them saying, "But it was the greatest adventure ever, Mom. And you know how much you encourage our adventures." This would soothe Mom's feelings for awhile until the next time she started thinking about how dangerous the Mustang Roundup had been.

Reality set in as the kids had to settle into their summer chores working around the cabin. Every morning Mindy was up early and dove into her chores like a cyclone. She usually finished up and arrived at Hi-Lonesome by noon. After lunch, she would head out with Charlie and Tomás to work with the Mustangs.

It was a slow process. First, they had to win the trust of the wild Mustangs. The horses only knew the fear and flight response. They spent a week in the corral walking around and just getting the horses use to their presence. Tomás had informed Mindy, during their training, that he had chosen the name Warrior for the big black stallion.

Since Tomás lived at the ranch and had more time to train his stallion, he was further along than Mindy was with her mare.

Discouraged, Mindy felt like she was stuck on the second step of Charlie's training. But three long afternoons later, Mindy's mustang finally let her draw close without running away. As the horse came near, Mindy would look her mare in the eye and then turn around and walk away. A few days later, the horse had started to follow Mindy. Two days after that, she would allow Mindy to gently pat her.

"Here we go, Windy Girl," Mindy said to the mare she had named after watching the wind toss her mane and tail the first day in the corral. She gently rubbed all around the horse's ears. Then she patted the mare all over, touching her back, sides, withers and legs.

"Good job!" Charlie smiled. "See how she lets you do that? It shows she is getting familiar with you."

At the end of the day, Mindy and Tomás would sit around and compare notes about how their training was going. Sam and Rip joined in sometimes with their own stories about the horses they were working with.

Even Grandpa would sit and listen. His eyes were always on Mindy as she described her day. She would catch him looking at her and wished she knew what he was thinking.

The next week, Tomás was up on Warrior riding bareback. "When asked, Tomás explained that riding bareback was part of the traditional training regimen they used back in his country. Charlie still had his doubts about this new technique, but he had to admit that Tomás had made it look easy and the stallion seemed to be responding.

Each time the horse started bucking, Tomás hung on to his mane.

When the horse reared up, Tomás would slide off, calm Warrior down and talk quietly to him. Finally, the black stallion allowed Tomás to sit unmoving on his back. The next challenge was to walk him around the corral.

Mindy could hardly believe it when she arrived at the ranch one day, just in time to see Tomás and Warrior riding out toward the north range. Mindy stood with her hands on her hips. If truth be told, she was jealous that he was able to ride his stallion like that. "Hey," she yelled.

Tomás waved and gave a thumbs up, but kept riding away from her.

"Come on, Mindy," Charlie said as he grabbed her hand and pulled her toward the barn. "Today is going to be a busy day for you, so let's get going."

Charlie had taught Mindy that horses, like people, get bored doing the same training over and over again. So, she started out by walking towards Windy Girl and then they fell in step together as the horse trailed her around the corral. Finally, she stopped. The horse stood still slightly behind her. Mindy turned and stepped to the left of the horse as she gently slid on her halter. This halter training had proven difficult for both of them but had gradually become the easiest part of their daily routine.

Charlie called her over and they discussed tips on getting the mare familiar with the saddle. After resting a few minutes, Mindy drew a deep breath and carried the blanket and saddle into the corral and set them down.

While the horse was standing still, she looked her in the eyes and chatted quietly for a moment.

Picking up the blanket, she rubbed Windy Girl with it. She then unfolded it and gently slid it on her back. The next step was to pick up the saddle and set it on her back. Mindy steadily placed it in the correct position as the mare's ears pricked up and flicked. Mindy rubbed the horse all over and under her belly. Now it was time to cinch up the saddle. Charlie had warned her to be ready for her horse to buck. But Windy Girl had sat quietly as Mindy slowly tightened the cinch.

Mindy picked up the lead attached to the halter and walked around the corral. After a while she stopped and slid the saddle off.

"Now put the saddle back on and play with it, like I told you," Charlie instructed.

Mindy went through the steps to put the saddle on again and then bounced the saddle up and down on Windy Girl's back. She then flopped the stirrups against her sides and wiggled the saddle back and forth. Then she took it off and put it back on at least ten times. Windy Girl was alert and cautious, but held steady.

Later that afternoon, when the group got together to discuss their progress, Charlie said, "I have never seen a horse respond the way Windy Girl responds to Mindy. She has won that horse's trust, that's for sure."

Grandpa listened and harrumphed quietly under his breath.

The summer moved on and into the early days of August. By now, Tomás could saddle up, ride out and had the ranges of Hi-Lonesome to explore. Mindy was allowed to ride Windy Girl around the lodge, but she could only ride the far reaches of the ranch with Charlie.

One afternoon when Mindy had just arrived at Hi-Lonesome, a pickup truck pulled into the lodge parking. The summer had been filled up training Mustangs and with the many customers who had come and gone through Grandpa's training program. It had been a busy time. However, Mindy knew school was coming and Tomás would be leaving soon.

She was thinking on these things, when the cowboy from the pickup walked up and asked if the boss was around. Mindy directed him to the barn where Charlie was working.

"Ah…what a beautiful black stallion," the cowboy said casually, as he changed course to where Tomás was working with Warrior.

Mindy felt something niggling at the back of her mind… something troubling about the man. Like a streak of lightning, it flashed into her head. He had a snake tattoo on his hand exactly like the one Joe had on his arm.

Mindy started running toward Tomás. "Tomás. Look out!" she yelled.

Tomás looked up, but he didn't understand the danger. As Mindy ran closer, she saw the cowboy reach behind his back where he had a gun stuck in his belt.

Tomás still did not realize the danger and no one else was around to help. "I'm gotta do something," she realized. "Without thinking, Mindy ran at him as hard she could, lowering her shoulder as she seen Josh do in football and hit him low in the legs.

"Oomph," he groaned as he went down hard. The problem was, Mindy had also hit the ground hard and had the breath knocked out of her. Even though Mindy knew she needed to call for help, she couldn't catch her breath.

Seeing Mindy flying through the air and the cowboy going down, Tomás finally got it! Something was wrong. He ran towards Mindy shouting for help. Charlie and Grandpa heard Tomás' shout and came racing out of the barn and found a heap of people on the ground. Tomás sat on top of the cowboy securing him to the ground. Charlie promptly tied him up while Grandpa called the sheriff. The sheriff's department, the FBI and Doc all arrived about the same time and the outlaw was carted off to the hoosegow. The final member of Sanchez's gang was behind bars and Tomás was safe to return to his family.

Josh could not believe that Mindy had brought the criminal down with a football tackle, but she had the cuts and bruises to prove it. "I just did what I have seen you do hundreds of times on the football field."

"Next time use pads," Josh instructed with a smile and gave her a small hug. He was feeling very proud of his sister, but a hug was all he could do to show it.

***

The last days of the summer, Mindy and Tomás were allowed to ride out together on their newly broken mustangs. But not too far, and always under the watchful eye of one of the ranch hands.

Mindy and Tomás were riding up to the barn about two weeks before he was set to return home. Suddenly, Tomás yelled in surprise, slid off his horse and ran towards a man who stood waiting with open arms. Father and son hugged as only Latinos can do.

Mindy tied up the horses and walked up to the group who now surrounded Tomás and the older man. She could easily guess who he was as he looked like an older version of Tomás.

"Mindy, this is my Father!" he exclaimed. "Y padre aqui es mi novia, my very best friend, Mindy." Tomás smiled at Mindy. Then he smiled at his father as he could feel the tears gathering.

Aunt Netta had a snack ready in the house, because she knew of the surprise visit of Senor Castillo. Later that night, Tomás and his father ate a Texas style steak dinner at the Cunninghams. Doc, Grandpa and Netta were there, of course, as Sherry always had plenty of food on her table.

The exchange of stories lasted late into the night. And in the coming days, both families traded their histories. Tomás and his dad heard all about the Cunninghams and their Magic Cabin adventures.

The Cunninghams learned about the history of Tomás' home in Maracabito and his family's centuries old role in it. Senor Castillo was a great story teller and painted a picture of the olden times and the struggles to make Maracabito a safer place to live. He told many stories of the beauty of the country, the people and their way of life.

That night Mindy went to bed feeling like she had made a visit to Tomas' country.

CHAPTER 20

MINDY'S WINS HER SPURS

Mindy and Tomás, joined by Shannon, spent the next few days riding together. They rehashed all the adventures they had shared that summer. Mindy was even taking notes to do an illustrated story of their summer.

There were trips into town for ice cream and the video arcade. Most nights they had a campfire supper with Doc, Charlie, Aunt Netta, and Grandpa. Both Mindy and Shannon's families joined in for these fireside meals. The ranch hands did the cooking over the fire for everyone, including the many guests that were staying at the ranch. The reputation of Aunt Netta's cooking and the campfire meals were a large part of the ranch's well known tradition.

Many days, Tomás and his father would ride off alone late in the afternoon. Other times, Mindy would see them sitting together in the rocking chairs on the porch of the ranch house, heads bent in serious conversation.

Mindy tried not to be jealous of their time alone. She knew that they needed to talk about many things. So she stayed away, helping Charlie in the barn or working with Windy Girl.

***

Four nights before Tomás was scheduled to leave, the three friends walked out from the lodge a half mile to a huge, solitary rock. A bull nearby eyed them menacingly, but they were too busy laughing and talking to pay him any attention. They climbed up to the highest point on the tall rock. It was work to get up there, but from the top you could see all of the ranch buildings, horses and cattle.

It was the perfect spot on the ranch to watch the sun set. Tomás opened Aunt Netta's picnic basket and passed out fried chicken, bread and butter sandwiches, grapes, and drinks. He dug right in.

"Where's the dessert?" Mindy asked. She looked in the bottom of the basket. No dessert there.

"I guess Aunt Netta forgot to put it in," Shannon said.

"She never forgets dessert," Mindy grumbled, picking at her chicken. Tomás and Shannon kept their eyes on the ground, not looking at each other. They were determined not to ruin the big surprise that was coming. Tomás and Shannon were glad to eat all that Aunt Netta had packed. But Mindy sat on the rock hardly eating anything.

"Just four more sunsets until you return to Maracabito, Tomás," Shannon said sadly. "Are you ready to go home?"

"Yes, I am, in some ways. I miss my family so much. And I have to go back to school, too." Tomás gave Mindy a friendly shove. "I know you're not too fond of school, Mindy, and you would rather be at the ranch all the time. I will miss the ranch, too. I told my father last night that I do not know how I will be able to live without my new American friends and Hi-Lonesome."

Tomás looked at Mindy's sad eyes. "My wise father said, 'You will get through it, Tomás. And…you can come back next summer if you want to!'"

"Really…you think you could?" Mindy asked breathlessly. "And would you want to?"

"I will if I am invited," he said with a smile. "Charlie said he would give me a job and…"

"Oh, that's awesome," Mindy said, with a tear sliding down her cheek.

The three sat quietly enjoying the sunset and being together.

"We'd better get back," Shannon said, giving Tomás a wink.

"Yes, and right now!" Tomás said. "Well, er…before it gets too dark." There was a surprise brewing that Mindy knew nothing about.

Mindy was not ready to go, but she had no choice. Shannon grabbed her hand and all three kids slid down the face of the rock.

When they walked up to the ranch house, Tomás stopped. "I like the way the lodge looks at night. All the lights hanging on the porch and the cheerful light shining out through the windows… lots to miss," Tomás said.

"Looks homey," Shannon agreed, as they walked inside.

The dining room was set with a large buffet. People staying at the ranch were in line or sitting at tables eating heartily.

The breakfast room had a sign stuck on the double French doors.

"Private Party -- No Entrance Please".

"I wonder what's going on in there," Mindy mused.

"Well, let's go in and see," Shannon said.

"But it says no…"

Josh opened the door and pushed Mindy inside. A large banner draped above the windows caught Mindy's eyes. "MINDY WINS HER SPURS." Surrounding these words were pictures of spurs and mustangs.

"Grandpa has a few words to say to you, Mindy," her dad said as he came up and guided his speechless daughter to a chair at the center of the table. Shannon and Tomás were seated on either side. All her friends were there. Doc, Charlie, Aunt Netta, the ranch cowboys, and her family, were all seated at a long table. Tomás' Dad and Shannon's family completed the group.

Grandpa walked up and stood at the head of the table. "Mindy," he said in his gruff voice. "A while back I said I wasn't sure whether you could win your Grandmother and Great Grandmother's spurs. But I seriously underestimated you.

Mindy sat wide-eyed at the table and looked at her grandpa. She realized his gruff voice was not because he was grumpy, but rather because he was trying to remain unruffled.

"I also said that I didn't know who would present these spurs to you if you happened to win them." Grandpa cleared his throat and continued on.

"I am right proud to say that your skills have given me a new perspective. You won these spurs fair and square. Not only did you help on the mustang round up, but you have trained your mustang, Windy Girl, as well as any trainer could have."

"Even more important, you rode through all kinds of danger with Tomás, and played a large part in keeping him from being kidnapped. Grandpa was quiet for a moment and then wiped his nose on his sleeve. "So I am mighty proud to be the one to present you with the Cunningham family spurs."

Grandpa walked over to Mindy and handed her the spurs. After a shy hug, he went back to his seat and sat down.

Everyone clapped and cheered. And then Charlie, Tomás' dad, Shannon, and Aunt Netta had to have their turn to praise Mindy's hard work.

Then everyone started talking about Tomás and Shannon's part in the summer adventures. They were both honored with words of admiration and hugs. Finally, delicious cakes (made by Aunt Netta, of course) were brought out and set on the buffet. "Your dessert," Shannon and Tomás laughed teasingly.

"Now I see," Mindy laughed. "I knew there was no way that Aunt Netta would had forgotten dessert."

There was one cake for each kid. Shannon took out her camera and took pictures of each cake. Tomás' cake was decorated with his black stallion and Mindy's cake had grandma's spurs.

The laughter and party went on...well, as they say in the country, "*until the cows came home.*" Finally, everyone began to head out. Charlie and the kids had decided to sleep outside. No sooner had they flung their bedrolls on a grassy spot close to the barn, they had climbed in and went fast to sleep.

***

Three days later everyone went to the airport to see Tomás off. With goodbyes and lots of hugs, Tomás slowly followed his father down the ramp toward their private jet where his black stallion had been carefully loaded into a special stall for air travel. He turned around and tossed a cheerful wave, but it was clear to see that he had tears in his eyes. The girls were also sniffling as they stood close by each other's side holding hands.

And then Tomás was gone.

And then the Summer's Adventure had come to a close.

And then school started.

***

Karilynn was pleased to return to school and see her friends.

Josh was enthusiastic about the start of another football season.

And Mindy…Mindy tried not to be cross about going to school. Shannon did her best to cheer her friend up. "Let's make a journal about our summer adventures." Starting with Mindy's notes, they wrote an exciting story of the best summer ever. Mindy added pictures she had painted and some sketches she had drawn. It was a slow process, but by October they had finished and mailed a copy of _Tres Vaqueros_ off to Tomás.

***

Like it or not, the school routine began. Herm was not there anymore and Germ seemed to have lost his nerve for bullying.

Outdoor school was coming soon. "We had a great time last year, didn't we?" asked Principle Noble with his hand to his ear. The students whistled and clapped. "This year all the grades will work hard to reclaim the forest that was damaged in the fire." Mr. Noble patted his stomach, obviously pleased with himself and his idea.

After school, the kids loaded up on the bus with Mr. Wooley, who was in a better mood now that Herman Prinz had been shipped back to his parent's embassy in Washington D.C. Mr. Wooley personally thought he should have been sent to jail, but then again, Washington D.C. was no great place to live either.

***

However, what really saved Mindy's spirit, was Saturdays at Hi-Lonesome ranch. She and Shannon helped Charlie in the mornings with Riding School. And then Mindy would hang around in the afternoons working with the kids who came with their parents to learn to train their own horses.

One evening over dinner, Mom surprised the family by announcing, "Guess who's coming to dinner on Friday night? Grandpa and Aunt Netta are going to join us for a family evening." Dad and the kids looked surprised at the announcement.

"I think Mindy has won him over," Dad said with a smile.

"The problem is, I have no idea what to fix for them. Considering how good a cook Aunt Netta is, I want it to be something special."

"Why don't you fix your great chicken and dumplings? They'll love that," Dad said encouragingly. Mom's answer was a face that continued to show her indecision.

Friday evening finally arrived and Grandpa and Aunt Netta were ushered into the living room for a glass of wine.

Before long, Mom called them all in for dinner. She served her famous chicken and dumplings with homemade rolls, ears of Olatha corn, and green beans smothered with onions and bacon. For dessert, she served banana pudding and cherry cobbler.

"Where did you learn to cook like this?" blurted out Grandpa, as Aunt Netta looked on with a huge smile.

"All us Texas gals know how to cook from birth," Sherry replied, as she gave him a big grin, "and we love to see folks enjoying our Texas cuisine."

"Well, that must be it then," Grandpa replied, with a shadow of a grin.

The mood around the table gradually relaxed as Mom served up coffee and dessert. Josh and Dad chatted about Monte Vista's upcoming football season and Grandpa joined in.

"Mindy, Tomás told me you're quite the artist," Grandpa said turning to her. After looking at some of your work, I totally agree with him. I was wondering, Dan, could I talk with Mindy about some pamphlets I need help with?"

"Of course," Dad replied.

"Mindy, would you join me in the living room?" Grandpa asked her. Mindy looked over at Mom, who gave her a small nod.

"Yes sir," Mindy replied reluctantly. She still didn't know what to expect from her "new" Grandpa.

Grandpa sat in the big overstuffed chair next to the couch where Mindy was sitting. The fire in the fireplace was burning bright and made the room feel warm and friendly. However, Grandpa and Mindy didn't feel the coziness as they both felt ill at ease and nervous.

Mindy stared at the flames as Grandpa fumbled for the right words. "I'm not a big talker as everybody knows," muttered Grandpa.

"That's an understatement," Mindy thought. She would have laughed out loud, but that would have only made things worse. Instead she answered, "Yes sir," and continued looking into the flames.

Grandpa cleared his throat and said, "I was wondering if you could use your artwork to help me with a project?" Mindy dared to move her eyes from the fire to Grandpa's face and found that his eyes were watching her. "Here's the deal," Grandpa said. "The Hi-Lonesome Ranch needs some new pamphlets…er…brochures as Aunt Netta calls them. I was wondering if you could do the artwork for them?"

"I don't know if I could, but I'd sure like to give it a try," Mindy replied with a hopeful smile.

"Here's what I'm thinking." Grandpa said, as he reached into his back pocket and pulled out some folded up papers. "Come over here and have a look."

Mindy walked over and sat down on the arm of the big chair.

"This is the old one," Grandpa said, handing her a pamphlet. "This is what I don't want. What I do want is some new ideas from you and here are some thoughts I'd like to see in a new brochure. After allowing her some time to look through it, Grandpa asked, "What do you think, Mindy?" He was even smiling.

Photos of the ranch, sketches of horses and types of training were all listed. "I think I can do this," Mindy answered excitedly. "I already have some thoughts." They put their heads together and started talking about some new ideas.

***

As you may have already guessed, this idea came from Doc, when Daniel had asked him for some help on how to be a better grandfather. It had taken a lot of courage for Grandpa to come over for dinner and ask for Mindy's help. "I'd rather ride a bucking bronco than ask for help." But once Grandpa set his mind on something, he followed through with it.

Fifteen minutes later, they stood up and shook on it. Grandpa got quiet again and seemed to struggle for words. He patted

Mindy on the shoulder and said, "you know, I would like to be a better"…he choked up as Karilynn rushed into the room and threw her arms around him. "You're the best Grandpa in the whole world."

"Well…thanks," was all Grandpa could say to the two girls.

"Come on, Grandpa," Karilynn said, grabbing his hand and pulling him into the kitchen.

"Need some more pie, Daniel?" Mom asked innocently, as Grandpa quickly found his coat and made a beeline for he front door.

"I guess not, Sherry. Getting late for us old folks, you know."

The whole family waved goodbye from the front porch as Grandpa and Aunt Netta made their way up the dark road.

Mindy walked back into the house and sat down in front of the fire. "I just love our fireplace," she said with a happy smile.

***

Just about the same time all the Cunninghams were feeling peaceful and contented in the Magic Cabin, Moose, bear and bees were racing through the woods towards Doc's cabin. As they approached Doc's place, they slipped behind some towering blue spruce to listen to a conversation taking place on Doc's front porch. The wind blowing toward them from the creek brought the agent's words to their ears.

Doc had just arrived back home and was once again conversing with the FBI agent he had met earlier in the summer.

"You've got to be on the alert, Dr. Stephens," the FBI agent spoke forcefully. "We have heard that rogue agents want the secrets you've got and are closing in, determined to retrieve them."

"I knew this time might come," Doc said calmly. "I will keep an eye out for them. You know Killer is always here to protect me," he said as he leaned down to scratch Killer's ears.

The agent cautioned, "Be careful, be very careful, these are desperate times."

"I will," Doc replied, "and if Killer and I round up these traitors, you'll be the first to know."

As the agent drove away, Killer and Doc went back inside.

Manners Moose brumbled, "Here we go again, we'll have to risk hoof and horn to bring things aright."

Responding to the agent's warning, BF Bear simply said, "Whoa… another adventure is on the way."

THE END